The Dowry

a novel

Michael J. Nercessian

ISBN (paperback): 979-8-9854659-2-1
ISBN (ebook): 979-8-9854659-3-8

For Alec and Cassie –
Follow your dreams…fly!

In nature there are no rewards or punishments:
there are consequences.

Horace Annesley Vachell, *The Face of Clay*

Talis

It became fashionable to wear your uterus and developing fetus on the outside, slung over your shoulders like a gaudy designer carry-all, a swishing, gurgling accessory to any dinner outfit. Known as an "outie"—slang for Outer Uterus Terrarium—these pregnancies were an endless source of pride for the beaming couple and a not-so-subtle signal to society that they'd arrived. If I'm given permission to birth a child, if I ever arrive, I'm certain to follow a more traditional path—an "innie"—like my mother and my grandmother and my great-grandmother. Madness, a true, palpable madness is so close to normal, you never see it coming.

Talis
(The Moon)

What is it about the night moon that encourages such foolish dreams? Or does it conjure the dreams of fools? And why does the moon conspire to conceal the scarred and pitted backs of our collective deception? There's a question! Often our dreams are a product of an unyielding algorithm. Sometimes it's the opposite. Only the cunning and the bold can decipher which is which and when is when.

The night wind, warm and sweet, carried a mild scent of fresh ozone. Despite the warmth of the wind and a glass of tepid absinthe in my hand, I shivered under greyish-blue moonlight. The damp night grass crept into the dark spaces between my toes, aiding my shiver, my discomfort. I squirmed in the chair unable to find a comfortable bend to my back. There was a time when I didn't drink, when absinthe held no appeal, but the days were different then, more innocent. Now I sat, my neck wrenched into an impossible question mark shape, my eyes wide, staring upward.

The moon was my escape when sleep eluded me, especially when I was young. It held the infinite promise of far-flung places where dreams deftly elbowed troubles aside and adventure awaited at every rocky turn. When I looked up, I wondered if there was someone looking back at me, someone just like me, dreaming of their own far-flung adventure on our blue marble, our sightlines crossed somewhere in the dark frontier. Sometimes, I'd get lost in thought for hours, curled up with a damp, fraying wool blanket on a backyard chair, my father emerging from the house to collect me in the middle of the night.

"Talis," he'd say softly. "It's time to take your dreams to bed. The moon will still be there tomorrow."

Then he'd pick me up, my body pliable and warm under the blanket, my knees folding over his forearm, and carry me into the house…to my bed. Only then, after being rescued, would I sleep soundly…dreamless.

Despite my father's assurances, the moon wasn't there for many more tomorrows, at least not the innocent, alluring moon of my childhood. This adult moon proved to be a leaking, unseaworthy ship, rudderless and doomed. Even the rats couldn't abandon the listing vessel in time and they drowned a rat's death. It's taken sixty years to convince myself the night sky still possesses those wondrous wonders of my youth. My opinion of the moon remains a work in progress, dithering in a grey periphery between pious conviction and a heretic's ungainly rage.

Reaching the stars, and especially conquering the moon, was long a measuring stick of our collective mitigation of nature. From the moment we craned our necks upward to form that very same question mark, we aimed our curiosity toward those heavens, vast and, as far as we knew, unbounded. The first moon landing—men in tinfoil suits dutifully planting the flags of dead republics—was hailed as a great success thousands of years in the making. It had all the qualities of a fine dream.

That was until Pride, the first lunar settlement—or at least the first civilian settlement. Within months, ten thousand men, women, and children were lost when the oxygenation system failed. Then the back-up systems failed. Then the escape vehicles, already in short supply, failed in fiery glory. We'd learned surprisingly little from the Titanic. In a heartbeat, or rather a ceasing of heartbeats, we were forced to accept that we just weren't ready. Pride. Throughout time, humans have shown uneasiness with humility and a comfort with deception.

My father, the dutiful citizen, volunteered to lead a reclamation team sent to Pride. They had the unenviable task of gathering the dead with hooks and nets and vacuums. I'll never forget my father's face the day he left for the moon, his skin pale as the moon itself, his eyes reddened, clammy around the edges, like he'd lost something. Like something had been stolen from him.

"The moon," he said before hugging me tighter than I ever remember. "Is still a place of wonder and magnificent potential. Don't lose faith in it even though others will."

When my father arrived on the moon, victims still hovered aloft in the thin atmosphere, eyes wide open, their lives forever paused. Some were vaporized, instantly lost to time. There were some who'd suffocated while still strapped into the escape pods, eternally silent, yet properly secured and fluent in the safety procedures they'd recently been read.

The bodies, the ones they recovered at least, were identified and categorized, coded and clustered by family, loaded into capsules and entombed in holes bored deep into the moon rock. My father's team attended the ceremonies, seeing them off, but there were few others save military units and security personnel. The tears (and there were tears) were more for us than for them—more for the living than the dead.

In the weeks and months following the disaster, there were no civilian transports to Pride. Entire generations of families had stood tall to make Pride their home. Now, there'd be few remaining on Earth who remembered them. There was simply no one left to grieve.

The reports, conclusions and causes were buried along with the flesh and bone. It was recommended there be no formal recommendations. Before long, the faucet of rumors and gossip squeezed to a trickle, then a drip, settling into gentle whispers behind cupped palms. Soon no one was talking about Pride. It was neither introduced into school curriculums nor offered a day of remembrance or anniversary. Within a year it was a mere shoulder shrug to history like it had never happened.

One night on what would be the anniversary of Pride, my father and I were seated across from each other in the backyard, absorbing rays of moonlight with our naked faces.

"One way or another, they were never meant to come home," my father mused, his head shaking with that melancholic disbelief reserved for those who spend their lives knowing better.

He never fully recovered from Pride nor forgave himself for his role. My father was a man of many regrets.

I've never forgotten those words: "…they were never meant to come home."

—

My father died on a Tuesday, two years shy of his one hundred-thirtieth birthday. Until the very end he received the best care, but nothing took, and there was little measurable improvement. The plans, the strategy sessions, and tactical maneuvers continued to unfold until the shelf of potions and pixie dust was bare and his spirit worn thin. Along the way, his body flatly rejected the replacement organs grown for him: a bladder and liver. The replacements for the replacements suffered the same fate. His body dissolved them into a gritty mush before the stew was absorbed into his bloodstream. The organ stew required a full blood filtering and sterilization—an unpleasant process even for the willing. In the end, he asked us to let him go and we did.

As is tradition, his body was liquefied and recycled, then fed into the energy generation system via pumps and tubes and funnels. He was a traditionalist at heart and would have wanted it that way. Even if he didn't, it was too late. What was done, was done. Near the end, when his eyesight was fading and the clock had lost its way, he said, "Talis, I always thought I'd die while we were camping. That was how I planned to go. Blinded on my own terms, by my own hand." Only now, all these years later, do I understand the significance of his "own terms." Unlike the life he led, he died a humble man.

My father had a big, booming laugh best described as a vibrant, but nervous tick. He'd make a statement and let loose that wonderful laugh, the sound enveloping my ears and shaking the very ground we stood upon. I never understood what was so funny, why he laughed in those moments, but his laugh made me smile. Now, it too was gone. That's the uncomplicated way I hope to remember him.

Unplanned death was so infrequent it lost the charm of its ancient personification of black, hooded cloak and scythe, boney white hands and face steeped in shadow. There was simply no need. Instead of a terse, gravelly voiced specter, death had morphed into a crooning court jester, a harlequin, a fraud. Some, the ones who claimed Pride was either a hoax or conspiracy, grew arrogant enough to claim we'd vanquished the very specter of death, placed it under our miraculous, opposable thumb and outrun something we ultimately knew we couldn't outrun.

Death itself wasn't a somber and sudden stop. The end of the line was an intricately choreographed affair often years in the making, a subtle, unnoticed drip in time filling the black kettle until the top was finally breached and time began to overflow. There were few surprises. Even the immeasurable failure of Pride with ten thousand dead at the snap of the boney finger happened far beyond our sight-line. It didn't appear real or unplanned or important. It was, however, real to my father and he went to his own grave having never fully balanced the account.

I wonder what color eyes death, the real death, not the jester festooned in tights and a belled hat, would choose if ever he could fold down his sooty hood and reveal his true self to us. Yellow, I think—the yellow eyes of a murderous and unrepentant tabby on the prowl. My father had yellow eyes though the color was not of his own choosing and he couldn't have known death would fancy it. And, yes, death is likely a he. I've found women want to renew life while men are intent on ending it.

The small wooden table next to my chair listed to one side, its spindly legs wobbly on uneven grass, barely holding the weight of the glass I set down. The absinthe had cooled and a thin, cloudy-white layer swirled clockwise on the surface. A small black fly circled my head, then dove out of the moonlight and commenced a backstroke in the thickening liquid. With a flick of my wrist, I emptied the contents of the glass onto the lawn. In the loneliness of night, the poured liquid sounded like a full mop bucket being unceremoniously expelled onto a dingy city sidewalk at dawn.

My neck ached from the contortions of my curiosity. I shivered again. It was a fear shiver, fickle, slightly reckless—I recognized it immediately. I checked the time: 11:45pm. At the turn of the day, the flipping of the calendar to the fifth day of the new year, my stomach would turn sour, devouring itself from the inside, and my throat would fill with acid and bile. Like last year and the year before and the year before that, the same fear, almost a friend to me, returned on this day as I awaited news. Somehow, I'd convinced myself this year (like I did every year) would be different. This would be the year. My year. Our year. Our arrival. It was all a facade, of course. Hope, like life on the moon, remained in short supply.

On the fifth day of the new year, for the past eighty-five years, applicants received official word on the device via secure channel. The lucky were granted as much relief as joy on this day: a deep exhale, vindication, validation, a greater purpose—humanity itself. If there was ever a time for hyperbole, this was the time. It remains unclear how many of us were considered "lucky" in a given year.

The number of arrivals, in the depths of my imagination, was tightly controlled by some feckless, dour accountant seated in a cramped office with the door locked and yesterday's cup of coffee forming a sticky, brown ring on his desk. These numbers were not for public consumption or public speculation. Like gossip, public estimation was considered bad form. A quick, mental count of my friends and acquaintances suggested the vast majority were among the unlucky, among those still burdened. Or maybe I was the only one alone in the darkness, adrift with wind, still seated in my rickety chair awaiting a blessing. Even the moon could no longer light my way.

My mother confided the fifth day of her year was the greatest day of her life. My father said he was happy because she was finally happy. To celebrate, they took a ride to the mountains in a hulking, hydrogen-powered convertible my father kept in the garage for emergencies. A relic of another age, the boxy, marine-blue creature was passed down from my grandfather and hadn't left storage in many years. In the weeks leading up to the new year, my father cleaned and serviced it in the unlikely event of good news. My mother insisted on the white cloth roof being folded down so she could let the wind take her hair as it pleased, flying about until her ears popped and her hair was tangled into impossible knots. She told me she never felt so free.

When they returned from the mountains, they drove past the houses of everyone they knew, screaming at the tops of their lungs, my father slamming a flat, reddened palm against the car horn in celebration. It must have been a sight—the lumbering blue antique with rubber tires humming along, my mother giddy, beside herself, throwing her arms in the air with an unbridled, snorting pleasure. That was until they realized their joy was surely other's pain. They went home.

It was many years before anyone in my family received a message on the device that wasn't the most feared four-letter word in our language: *wait*. In time, my older sister, Anna, was blessed with arrival. Yes, my parents had been blessed twice, a stroke of good luck impossible to imagine these days without considering a hoax or conspiracy.

I'd say my mother died of a broken heart after my father

died, but that's too trite and also untrue. The heart, her heart, the replacement heart, wasn't broken just incorrectly fitted. The heart designed and grown for her was the wrong size, too large, and the wrong shape. Square peg, round hole. And once my father was gone, his influence (for whatever reason he wielded influence) waned. It was gone once he was gone, and soon she was gone, too. Perhaps the enemies he'd garnered over the years had the last laugh. Perhaps it was simply nature's way.

The rumor mill was always in full force as the fifth day inched closer. Outside the official channels, there was unfettered gossip (though they were careful to avoid using the term "gossip") claiming this new year would be different, new criteria were being considered, new resources developed and released, a higher number selected overall. The messaging, concocted internally by gregarious public relations types and bled outward to the assumedly gullible public, was designed to drive hope rather than fear, joy rather than shivers. In other words, it was an attempt to calm the masses and release some air from the inflating balloon before it burst. We were sure, no matter how creative and viable the new rumors were, none of it was true. Yet we clung to each word against commonsense, continued to reassure ourselves we were desirable enough, to capture that last bit of humanity before the well-honed and oiled axe dropped onto our narrow necks.

My birth best friend, Delius, was selected a few years ago and decided to birth a boy, Lazarus, in honor of my sister Anna's husband. Lazarus was a wonderful, yellow-eyed gift for the ages. As you might imagine, we were quite envious (jealous, really), but happy for her nonetheless. She was thrilled, of course, with her perpetual smile and engorged breasts, a face-full-of-pink, mirthful portrait of motherhood. She was what we all hoped to be. We faked our maudlin praise, our smiles, our delight. Each year it grew exponentially more difficult to be happy for the lucky and the connected.

We, Lark and I, submitted our application each season (complete and on-time) for as long as I can remember, dotting "i"s and crossing "t"s, nearly begging, but the return message was always the same dirty four-letter word and yellow light. We hadn't been denied or even "not selected." Worse, we were in a permanent holding pattern, the deep, pitted hollow of purgatory. Unsurprisingly, the process took a toll on our marriage. Though Lark loved me, he no longer liked me much. The feeling was mutual.

The next morning, I awoke in a tepid absinthe sweat, alone. Lark was already dressed and gone. A yellow light emanated from the device, spilling false sunlight onto the floors and ceilings of my bedroom, casting shadow puppets on the wall when I wiped the sleep from my eyes. The light was neither the friendly green nor the government red (the one we all secretly feared) —just yellow, a continuation of limbo, an apathetic and unemotional: "Wait." Another year.

And there was a message from Anna. "Talis," she said in that smugly confident, big sister-ese where she wasn't really asking a question, but making a soft demand. "Can we meet at the cafe?"

I consider myself an only child, though my parents would disagree. Or they would have disagreed were they alive. I have a sister. Had a sister. We didn't speak for a long time. Not a word. Not a quiet gesture or loud smile. Not a groan. She became a different person when she arrived— she became my father's favorite. She died a long time ago. Actually, she's not dead, though I killed her off for many years. Recently, Anna and I have become friends again, but we'll never be sisters.

Anna worked in the Birth Office—an irony not lost on those of us who remained unarrived. We were sisters, Anna and I, I tepidly (and conveniently) reminded her, but she told me over coffee there was nothing she could do to help. "Algorithms," she said and shrugged her shoulders like I should know better than to ask. "That's that." There was no escape from the cold efficiency of it all. Escaping from Anna's efficiency proved similarly difficult.

The café's coffee machine stretched for thirty feet. It was a monstrosity of tubes and cylinders, each pushing and pulling and pumping liquids, solids and steam through myriad filters, heaters, coolers, and protein enrichment infusers. The whirling staff of ten wore white lab coats that remained immaculate despite thousands of opportunities for staining:

brown and black and red. I imagined a meticulous costume master hiding somewhere behind a curtain, replacement lab coats in every size hanging on a rack, pressed and ready, waiting for their turn to shine. I admired their confidence and dedication, turning knobs and pushing buttons, pulling handles on cables, a keen eye measuring out each frothy serving. Whether it was real or imagined, they appeared so... content. At that moment, having such purpose would have made me happy. Content, I mean. Happy is different.

Yet, I couldn't shake the thought it was all so overly complicated. Such a simple task steeped in historical methodologies—brewing coffee—but modernization had erected this great beast to muddle what was easy, mostly to keep people employed and busy.

In the not-so-recent past, everything was mechanized, robots and machines churning out automated miracles—like coffee. But we learned the hard way, with rockets and lasers that when people are bored, when they have too much time on their hands, they only sit still for so long. Idle time ultimately leads to wars and we have enough war already. It's far better to have a human pulling a lever and pushing a button on a coffee maker than pulling a trigger or pushing a button from a military bunker. And there would never be a need for Echoes.

That said, the coffee was delicious. Soon the flavor quelled my wandering mind if only for the moment.

"I have a thought, though," Anna said, her brown hair swept down over her eyes and half of her face. She used both hands to tuck her hair behind both ears. I could see her eyes now, round and shiny, reddish brown, almost rust, irises in fields of pure white. One elbow, rubbed raw, dug into the tabletop and she placed her chin onto the palm of her hand. She'd paused like she was about to bestow a midnight epiphany, to grace me with *my* epiphany.

"There's an opening for a new position in my quad. It's a new department, brand new, stunning really, called Acclimation." There was an odd excitement and "hands on her hips" to her tone, like she'd pushed me from the path of a moving train and was awaiting due credit. Maybe she had.

"Never heard of it," I said as I tried to drift off to… somewhere. Despite the promise of an entire day's nutrients and the satisfying flavor, I'd already lost my taste for coffee.

"Of course not! It's brand new and I haven't told you about it yet," she said and laughed, leaning back in her chair and slapping the palms of her hands on her knees to indicate just "how silly" I was. Then her tone grew serious and slightly melancholy. "It may help a little, you know, mentally, while you wait for approval to have a child."

My body, loose and without structure, listed toward her, leaning from my seat to provide what little attention I could muster. My being, my mind, all of me, was exhausted. "Or you could pull some strings for me," I said only half-joking. Even to my ears, my words sounded listless, pathetic and, most of all, without hope.

"Yeah, well, there aren't any strings to be pulled on that subject, sorry," she said in that grating, matter-of-fact tone used at city hall when you leave one application question blank. "But, about the job, and you wouldn't have heard this and you didn't hear it from me, but a decision was made recently, real high up, the top, to begin reclaiming military assets instead of disposing of them."

"What does that mean?" I asked, but only out of boredom. I wasn't interested. "Equipment? Aircraft? Sounds fascinating. Who cares?" I probably rolled my eyes.

"No," she said. "Oh, no," and leaned in toward me. She continued, hot breathed, in something I can only describe as falling between a whisper and a hiss. "Soldiers. Echoes."

"Reclaim them?"

"Yes."

"And do what with them?"

"They'll enter society," she said like she was happy I finally asked the right question, allowing her to unlock the juicy, private thoughts of her teen diary. "Fill the unfilled jobs, especially the jobs no one else is willing to do. Whatever's needed, really."

"Are you serious?"

"Oh, very," she said with raised eyebrows and Anna's patented snarky indifference.

"Wait!" I said and rubbed my eyes with the palms of my hands. "What was the process? I mean, before this?"

"That's generally been a mystery, right?" she acknowledged. "Until now, the Echoes who weren't killed on the battlefield or in accidents were disposed of after their 'useful' years—given a sedative that made them fall asleep and stopped their heart. That was that. The bodies were recycled into fertilizer. Instead, after their time is served, they're going to enter society and live out their lives. Their life cycle is already accelerated due to stress, so the algorithm says it will consume only 40% of the resources typically required in a human life cycle."

"Right, yes, the fucking algorithms again," I said. "Wonderful."

The algorithm, to me, was no more a predictor than a guess or a chance spin of the roulette wheel. Of course, if, on the fifth day of one of these new years, it pointed in my favor, raised my name and I'd won handsomely, I'd consider it a great purveyor of truth. Life is often a reflection of the view from a particular seat.

"Humane really, if you think about it," she said and raised her hands into the air. Then added what turned out to be a life's irony, "These aren't my rules."

"Have they considered how difficult it might be for clones to transition from the military into society? And what about the people who now have a clone of themselves running around? How are they going to react? How can we control this?"

"That's a big misconception," she explained. "They're not clones—they're Echoes. Twins—one egg, split. Anyway, that's why we now have a Department of Acclimation and some jobs to fill. Interested?"

"When is all this starting?" I asked.

Anna smiled but didn't answer.

"Who authorized this?"

A grin. It was done.

I brought the nearly cold cup of coffee toward my lips but didn't drink. Instead, I held the ceramic cup motionless, halfway between my mouth and the table. I exhaled through my nose, an elongated, pithy release of breath. I began to sweat. My head pounded from the inside, like consciousness was attempting an ungraceful escape, ready to crack open my skull and make a run for the nearest exit. Then, I lashed out.

"Is this why no one's getting approved for children? The resources are already assigned?"

I tried to appear calm while my blood boiled in anger and fear and disappointment. In the moment, I couldn't help but stare at the long pink scar that began high up on Anna's forehead and faded, slightly, down by her eyebrow. It was a meandering, jagged trench that couldn't decide on a direction to take and, as a result, the wound itself had healed poorly. I'd been staring at the pink line for decades, wondering what ghosts and demons it conjured. What did Anna think about each morning when she faced the mirror and wiped sleep from the pits of her eyes? She withstood constant headaches, like the one I'd conjured today, with little complaint.

After the injury, she endured numerous operations, skin grown in a lab from extruded tree fibers and bee's wax was woven in then applied to the surface, microscopic layer by microscopic layer. These painful procedures (she told me they were painful) were insisted upon, again and again. Yet, perhaps due to the depth of the wound or its zigzagging nature, it never blended with its surroundings and the skin tone never quite matched. In the end, she decided to leave it alone to fester, to serve as a reminder of the delicate nature of family and, perhaps a reminder to the culprit that she remained steady-fast. Despite everything, she was still here.

In the café, Anna smirked to herself, crooked and sanctimonious, like she'd won whatever unnamed game we were playing, before her typically bright, ivory skin (other than the scar), grew ashen and dull. Small wrinkles formed at the outer corner of each eye. "You don't need to worry," she said like she understood the worry I carry. She took a sip of what I can only assume was cold coffee. "Your Echo, her name was Barbara and you won't bump into her. She's dead."

"They have names?" I asked.

Anna leered at me. "Of course they have names!"

She paused for a moment, then said, "I shouldn't have told you. Never tell anyone about Barbara. Promise me that."

"I won't tell."

"Promise."

"I promise."

"Good. I don't need a red light."

No, there would be no red light for Anna. She'd already basked in the glow of a lifetime's altruistic green.

Anger filled my body again, my soul, all of me as I thought about her life, Anna's life. Anna's perfect little life. Then it was over. The thoughts drained away and I fought remorse. I also fought weakness and weighty regret—it's for the feeble—not for me. It's for people like Lark who ask and question: where did everything go wrong? I've become adept at fooling myself.

Lark
(The Meeting)

I was dressed before the sun rose, long before Talis awoke, before the lemony yellow beaming from the device greeted her with the violent sourness of indifference. My exit from the house was quiet, exceptionally quiet, even for me. Me, the coward, quietly skulking and sneaking about, sliding out of the house unnoticed, like a seasoned thief.

I don't know how to talk to Talis about the fifth day of the new year. Maybe I don't want to talk to her about it. It's difficult to know the difference when your daily existence balances on a cliff's edge. I imagine her looking into the morning mirror, blue eyes and perfect olive skin, long strands of sandy hair falling over her face attempting to hide her. There would be no consoling her today. I'd tried, truly, many times over many years. This day is always the worst day of the year. Of course, tomorrow I'll say the same thing about that day and repeat the process for a week, a month, a year. Infinity. What's the difference? There's an old saying: "fingers to the bone." Sometimes there's just nothing left other than gristle and tepid memories of future's hope.

We've grown apart.

Soon after I arrived at the office—no, I shouldn't use that word—when I reached the office, my device came to life with colored lights and buzzing and making a fuss. Without fail, messages about couples arriving (though not many and fewer than in the past) and questions asking if we had. I knew what awaited me. With a sweep of my hand I erased the lot of them. What's the difference? My life will continue regardless, unencumbered, unchanged and…unhappy? No, that's not the case. Other than today. And possibly tomorrow. I sat at my desk, put my head down and attempted to concentrate on work. As usual, I got nothing done. As usual, there was really no work to do.

I took lunch at Café Drame, a fine spot in the same district as the office. It was a short walk, buried in the depths of the French district, a tidy place with only five tables, two parked on the sidewalk "with a view" according to the advert. The device reserved a sidewalk table for me once a week and that day was my once a week. As usual, Café Drame was filled with middle level office types like me, "Mid-Levs" for short. We're neither the movers nor the shakers, but we aren't in the basement either. The day smelled of spring, fresh, like the world renewed and, for some, it was. I ordered a soup at random, closing my eyes and gesturing toward whatever menu projection was in front of me.

While my soup cooled (did I really order ochre noodles?) and my mind wandered (I guess I did order ochre noodles), I caught a glimpse of her in the distance, a woman walking in reckless, loose circles and making little progress. "Delius!" I called out to her and waved my arms above my head like an idiot. She didn't respond. I'd like to believe I'm not so easily forgotten or overlooked, but the fifth day of the new year is not like other days. People's dreams are often crushed on that day. Perhaps her dreams were brutishly ground in a pestle and mortar on that very morning. Then again, Delius had already arrived years ago, so I can't explain her total preoccupation with…something that wasn't me. She wandered off without even a glance in my direction.

It's often surprising to catch of glimpse of yourself as the world sees you. At the table, I stared into my water glass as it delivered my unfiltered reflection back to me. I still had the thick brown curls of a young man, but the skin of my face appeared sallow, almost translucent, and the color of my eyes had lost their sparkle, settling into a flat, unspectacular rust. My formerly stately nose, too, was not what I expected - it was wide and flattish like a cobbler's shoehorn. I dismissed it all, of course, blaming the rounded water glass for playing tricks with light and warping perspective before attempting to convince myself I was as handsome as ever.

The next week, from my table at Café Drame, I saw Delius again, wandering the city, lost in thought like she'd misplaced something (or someone) and was delicately retracing every step, every foot of ground. She had this walk, a sultry, confident walk, smooth-shouldered and rhythmic, that couldn't possibly be duplicated—of that I was sure. And she didn't have a sister. This time, I leaped up from the table, purple napkin stuffed into my collar, bits of lunch spilling onto the sidewalk while my chair tipped over backward with a thud. I'd graduated from the petty idiocy of waving my arms to a full-on, complete buffoonery, one that garnered crunched eyebrows and thin-lipped sneers from my fellow Mid-Lev diners. If nothing else, we must continue to evolve.

Delius was, in many ways, the one that got away. She wasn't the "it" girl so much as the "what if" girl. When Talis and I met (the traditionalists would say we were "courting") and I was subsequently introduced to her circle of friends, I developed a crush on Delius—forbidden, yes, but deep and, often enough, all consuming. She felt the same way and there were a few evenings when we emptied our hearts over warm absinthe and more than a few when we gave into the temptations. Perhaps it was all made easier because we knew it couldn't be. Our time together was finite.

Even after we both married (to other people and not each other) and settled into our lives, I had difficultly extracting her from my thoughts. When times were good, I thought of her a little. When times were not, I thought of her often. Lately, times are not. In times like these, the latent "what ifs" grow louder and more demanding, less murky in their intent and expectations. One hundred fifty years—a lifetime—is too long to be haunted by regret. That's become clearer.

Let me explain—it wasn't always this way. Talis and I were deeply in love, we still are, or at least we love each other. Those seem like two different emotions after all these years. While courting, our initial DNA samples were well received and our education and cognitive scores were satisfactory.

Even our resource consumption profile, tricky business in the best of times, was within the acceptable range. We were certain to qualify for all of society's coveted benefits and privileges. In other words, once we were officially married and the requisite paperwork submitted, our arrival was all but assured. There was happiness for many years. Our time was near. A limp-wristed rubber stamp by a bored, anonymous civil servant was imminent. It had to be. Until letters and official enquiries remained unanswered and called favors to family and friends, colleagues— anyone—remained unfulfilled. Things can unravel in an instant.

I was happy for Delius when she told me she and her husband had arrived. Why wouldn't I be? At the time, I smiled widely during greetings and gave firm hugs, slapped backs, and offered a toast to the lucky couple at a swanky restaurant in the Italian district. Yes, I did my part, summoned my inner thespian to great effect and acclaim, throwing about heavy words of wisdom while earnestly honoring their sacrifices before taking my rehearsed, languid curtain call bow.

That night, Delius appeared slightly embarrassed by all the fuss, twisting in her seat during the weighty speeches and expensive wine, a modicum of guilt well blended with newly earned arrogance. The feeling, I assume an amalgam of relief and pity, sadly, remains foreign to me. Her shoeless foot set firmly against my shin under the dinner table, moving gently at uneven intervals, offered little reassurance.

Like most couples in our social station, once a few of our friends had been approved, the pressure for us grew exponentially. The ticking clock of the device (the yellow devil), which in the early years, when time was still a friend, was more a pleasant melody of bells being lightly rung, became a penetrating, beating drum, a deafening rival without ebb. For Talis especially, time became an all-consuming nemesis. Sleep was elusive (even for me) and marred by sweat and dark dreams that clung like they were awaiting a gratuity before fading off. There was no hiding from it. At night, as I rested my head on the pillow, I could hear my own pulse, swishing, racing at great speed to keep pace with my running thoughts. I spent many nights fighting the urge to feel sorry for myself. More often than not, I lost.

I didn't receive a call from Talis the day I went to the café and ordered the ochre noodles. And I didn't call her. There wasn't a need. Another year and Talis and I hadn't arrived. I know she blames me, with my deviated septum and receding gums, my family history of high cholesterol and my grandmother's jaunty laugh. I'm certain there are myriad imperfections in my being I can't possibly defend. The disappointment, the pressure, the stink of failure has destroyed us from within, beckoned a paralysis and nudging parasite, like a cicada killer wasp has deposited its impenitent egg between us while we slept. She just won't say it. And in this new job of hers, she's being so secretive and dishonest. It's like I don't know her anymore.

I do believe Talis still loves me though she doesn't like me very much.

(The Birthing Center)

The Birthing Center was oddly quiet save a developing raucous on the four-hundredth floor. The center was typically busy for only a few months each year and it was late in the season for arrivals—their numbers had dwindled to a mere few hundred per day and most of the staff were reassigned to centers with more pressing needs. The self-cleaning walls and floors had recently molted, the thin layer of membrane peeled and regenerated, leaving the interior glowing in sterilized bliss. Every corner of the building smelled fresh and clean like a life renewed.

Shrieks emanated from a birthing room on the four-hundredth floor, the sound spilling into the stark white hallway, echoing off the walls and floors, bouncing off the ceilings. They were sharp, soul-crushing wails that lingered in the air like the laugh of a peculiar and unpleasant odor. The source of the sounds wasn't a child, though two children took their first breath of air in that very room earlier that day. It was the unsettled shouts of the mother and father that filled the hallway, a bickering that showed no signs of abating. A birthing nurse stood in the room with her arms crossed tightly in front of her chest, her chin tucked low into her sternum.

"You pick one," the nurse said with a calm, rehearsed demeanor. "That's the agreement. We spoke about this only yesterday."

"Leave them both!" the woman in the bed screamed.

"We have to choose one," the children's father said to her.

"No! They can't have either! They can't have them!"

"The world needs soldiers," the nurse said. "We all have Echoes. We all do our part."

"I'll speak to her," the father said to the nurse, his smile grown less confident than even that morning.

The nurse slowly turned her head and looked at him with vague disappointment before offering a kind smile— one that had witnessed the same scene play out each day. "I'll come back in a few minutes."

When the nurse had gone, the woman in the bed grabbed him by the shirt and pulled him close. She began pleading.

"Take them both and run! Take our children. Leave now. Take them far away. Take them to the mountains."

"I'm sorry, that's not an option. We understood from the beginning, we agreed to this."

"I changed my mind! I'm not agreeing to it anymore."

"You have to be reasonable…if we don't choose, they will!"

She gestured her arms toward the children, "Bring them both to me. Let me hold them."

He picked them up from the warming cart, one, then the other, and placed them in her arms. She smelled the tops of their heads and gently kissed them. There was a momentary calm, but it didn't last.

"How can we choose?" she asked. "How can they make us choose? I'll never let go!"

"I don't know how we choose, but we must."

"Do I name them?"

"No, not until the choice is made. It will be easier once the choice is made."

"It's so difficult to tell them apart—we need to name them so we can tell them apart."

"I don't think we should name them yet."

"Look at their eyes. They have the same beautiful eyes."

"They are beautiful, orange as a setting sun," he agreed.

"Don't try to change the subject!" she scolded.

The nurse returned and stood in the doorway; her arms crossed again. She called him over with a stern twitch of her finger.

"I'll be back in a moment," he leaned in and whispered to his wife.

The nurse led him down the stark white hallway to a stark white counter with several screens attached to shiny metal arms.

"I need you to read and sign a few things. Please make sure you read each one."

He read and signed various documents and agreements, scanning his eyes for approval before moving to the next.

"I'm sorry," the nurse said. "There's so many that need

signing. This is a happy day for you and I have you away from your family. It won't take long, there's just a few more you need to read."

On the tenth one, he exhaled in frustration and glared at the nurse.

"Just a few more," she promised in her voice reserved for impatient children and poorly behaved family pets.

When he was done, he gave the nurse a half-smile and raised his hands in surrender.

"That's it?"

"That's it."

"I'm sorry it took so long," he said on his way back into the room. "Paperwork."

His wife lay back in the bed with her eyes closed, her breathing was rhythmic and soft. A thin strand of drool leaked from the corner of her mouth and formed a small, shiny droplet on her chin.

Her arms were empty.

One child slept quietly in the warmer.

Lark
(Luna Summer)

Talis and I met during what's colloquially known as Luna Summer. It was the summer of Pride, the first permanent moon colony or at least the first moon colony that was meant to be permanent. We were both at university (I was an eleventh year and she was an eighth) and applied for summer jobs working on phase two of Pride. This grand (but ultimately doomed) lunar experiment was expected to house 100,000 citizens when all phases were complete. Within three months of announcing the colony, all 100,000 spaces were reserved and deposits taken, people fell over themselves to secure their place. The moving companies and real estate agents made a killing—at least at the beginning.

That summer, phase one was nearing completion and phase two needed hands, even our soft, unskilled hands. Thousands of recruiters descended upon college campuses clawing and fighting for commissions like famished jackals—they needed workers for everything from moving freight to monitoring the vital signs of other staff. There were quality control jobs certifying cables and ropes, the tensile strength of metal screws, even the colorfastness of uniforms when exposed to sunlight penetrating the thin atmosphere. They needed cooks and janitors, roofers and social workers. As they discovered, recreating a society required a sizeable society. Boxes were checked and the checking of boxes itself was checked. Redundancy was redundant. They thought of everything—except the probability of failure.

The first time I encountered Talis was in the waiting room of some thin-skinned, cold-handed doctor during the initial onslaught of tests, the endless poking and prodding required of the selection process. She was seated in a corner of the nearly empty waiting room, aloof and introspective, head down, like someone who wanted to be left alone. I was never one for social cues, so I sat a few feet away, rocking back and forth in my seat and humming nonsensically, making a general spectacle of myself. She tried to ignore me, but I have a presence, like a subtle but lingering odor you can't quite identify.

The first thing I noticed was her skin. She had wonderful skin. Unlike the sallow covering stretched over my bones, she had a smooth, light olive complexion like the sun had offered a gentle kiss one spring morning, but was too shy and respectful to court her further. Her hair kept falling over her eyes and narrow nose (that curls up a little at the tip). She used one hand to sweep her hair back over her forehead only to have it fall again. She repeated this gesture over and over, blue eyes intermittently shining through like a beacon to a lost soul. I found myself staring at her, mouth open (again, not one for social cues)—I couldn't help myself.

She was well aware of my lurid glare. She shifted her body away from me, turned in the chair and aimed her head toward a baleful, empty corner of the room with its baleful, empty promises. If she could have reduced and reformed her body into a wedge shape, transformed into the comical slice of yellow Swiss Cheese in those ancient cat and mouse cartoons, I have no doubt she would have before impolitely squeezing herself further into that corner. Such was the full discomfort of my presence.

I may have said "Hi," or "Hello," or another form of innocuous, uncreative greeting. It's possible I just grunted. Realizing she was the only one within the stark white waiting room (and, therefore, most likely the focus of the greeting), she reluctantly craned her neck in my direction and offered a quick, pained smile before curling into a tight ball on the chair, her knees pulled up against her chest and her arms wrapped around her shins. The nervous tapping of my feet against the tile floor did little to break the tension.

Over several weeks, we were examined for balance, heart rate, blood pressure, lung capacity, muscle strength, bone density and, most importantly, psychological well-being. The colony jobs were notorious for causing dramatic, very public mental breakdowns: "moon fever" and "lunar flu" were common slang. It wasn't surprising. Workers were required to spend ten-to-twelve-hour shifts zipped and pinned and fastened inside heavy, pressurized suits while tethered to beams or heavy equipment by rope and cable.

The conditions required workers to relieve themselves (all digestive systems, not just the convenient ones) while wearing suits sealed to keep everything outside, out and everything inside, in—and the worker meals from the cafeteria were notoriously unreliable. Pride workers battled everything from claustrophobia to urine induced skin rashes, sleep disorders to motion sickness.

Several (apparently) distressed workers untethered their own safety cables and floated into the darkness of space, spinning and squirming like spiders flushed down a drain. A few others used utility knives to make purposeful cuts in their protective suits, depressurizing them before their organs exploded like kernels of popping corn in an old-fashioned microwave oven. There were others too disturbing to mention. Yet, despite all the gossip and clear warnings, we couldn't wait to go on an adventure to the moon.

Neither of us was selected for on-site Pride work assignments. Neither would have the adventure we sought. Or we thought we sought. Perhaps it was for the best.

While awaiting our test results, Talis was more nervous than I was, gritting her teeth and biting her lower lip, her thumbs twirling in simultaneous, nervous ovals. As with most aspects of my life at that age, I projected as someone broadly apathetic, neither particularly interested nor against the prospect of working on the moon colony. I digested my results ("try again next year." a curious precursor to "wait") with a shoulder shrug and curled lip. As for Talis, her disappointment was more evident, a deep sigh and exhale, pushing her hair back over her head with one hand to reveal her swollen cheeks and reddened eyes. But her disappointment lay less in not landing the actual job, not on missing the adventure and more in the company she was hoping to keep.

At the time, Talis wasn't interested in me (this seems to be a theme). Her attention was focused squarely on Anna's husband, Lazarus, the handsome lunar cartographer and, ultimately one of Pride's founding staff. His skills and expertise were critical to the success (ahem) of Pride. He was selected for the initial team sent for a six-month civilian trial run. Lazarus was a dreamer, a star-gazer, his neck perpetually craned upward toward the heavens, never down at his feet. His mind was always somewhere far away. He was clumsy and distracted, tripping over sidewalks and spilling whatever liquid was poured into his glass—at times soaking the very paper he'd sketched a map upon while ignoring a lecture or feigning interest in dinner conversation. Perhaps that was the attraction for Talis—his body was here, flesh and bone, but his mind, his intellect, was firmly on the moon.

Lazarus was stationed on Pride at the end…his end… all of their ends. Talis' father told Anna he would personally conduct the search for him. On day two of the recovery, he found Lazarus strapped into an escape pod, bags thoughtfully packed and stowed like he'd won an all-expense paid pleasure cruise and was looking forward to a well-earned vacation. The twenty people aboard the pod suffocated while a golden voiced recording pleasantly delivered the vehicle's safety procedures. As designed (perhaps the only thing on Pride that worked to design), the pods monitored the internal oxygen levels and, when they registered a critically low level for too many minutes, the system released a sweet potion of carbon monoxide. It was a chemical parachute for the passengers. Their lungs gobbled it up like candy. They never left the dock.

In the moment, the end, the situation was clear to Lazarus. It must have been. The colony was imploding around him—they couldn't breathe and fires consumed any excess oxygen—and there was no rescue mission, no contingency plan from Earth. They were on their own and it all went wrong. His end came quickly and likely painlessly, "like dozing off after a good meal." At least that's what Talis' father told her and Anna while seated across from them at the kitchen table, his hands folded tightly in front of him, his eyes stoic and pious, like a man who was adept at delivering bad news. What else could he say? And there were no second chances. Lazarus would not have his Christ.

I allowed Talis her sanitized version of the death of Lazarus, a romanticized version of the captain and the sinking ship, maybe even a hero's death. Why wouldn't I? In truth, there were no pods that did not burn and no carbon monoxide systems to ease their pain. There were no soft landings. All were lost. No one, nothing was spared. In other words, there was no falling asleep to dreamland, no counting of sheep and waking up on the other side—whatever and wherever that may be. Any news of "dozing off after a good meal" was a ruse. Lies. If Lazarus hadn't found a way to take his own life with disaster closing in, to find a tidy ending before being choked and incinerated by his own dream, then I feel for him. The death awaiting him was wretched and painful, the stuff of nightmares, not dreams. It would have been for all of us had we been there.

Yet would it have made a difference in my happiness? Is a short, happy life better than a long life unfulfilled? Was Lazarus the lucky one?

I've often wondered if her father influenced Talis' application that summer, had it buried under the crush of other willing collegians or deleted by a shirt-pocketed, pre-pensioner seated at a lonely basement desk. That would make sense now. He had more influence than he let on—a man who required little ego, but garnered reverence and action with a simple look or nod of the head, an innocent wave of his hand. You had to pay attention to catch the nuance, to watch people who appeared not to know him catering, scrambling about to please him. It existed in plain sight, but you had to look carefully. Some say it's the best place to hide things. Her father was not who he said he was.

As for me, like many aspects of my life, I was, simply (thankfully), superfluous. They didn't need me and I didn't need them.

The destruction of Pride was witnessed by billons over the device before the feed was cut. It all happened at such extraordinary speed, mere seconds, a death vacuum. There was no warning, no time to send help. No time for them to help themselves.

A lifetime is counted in decades, happiness is counted in years, sickness is counted in months, tragedy is counted in seconds. Death is when the count ceases.

What was the collective damage of Pride? How many

billions questioned their choices, their station, their very existence? We're a generation of guilt. Then it was all forgotten, the corner of the rug was lifted and all was swept under.

Lark
(My Harriet)

It would be difficult to confuse Delius with another. Adding to the allure of her walk, her curly brown hair bounced with each voluptuous step, caressing down to the small of her back, catching my willing eye with each sway of her hips. And there's no confusing her eyes with those of another. They're a succulent, windy mauve, at once warm and inviting yet possessing a hint of danger. "A hint of danger"…that sounds silly to me, like I was wishing it into being. Was that what attracted me to her—some element of potential danger that I'd likely invented in my head? Was it a deep seeded want of adventure on my part—to ride off into a perverted sunset on horseback with the girl with the mysterious mauve eyes? They say the century mark, one hundred years old, usually ushers in a mid-life crisis, a ticking-clock breakpoint. Tick-tock. Perhaps I'm due. Though that would do little to explain our unsavory past.

Though it may appear suspicious, a ruse, a well-planned and plotted meeting of chance, I didn't go to the café to look for her that day. Not that I'm above such things—it just happens that this was not one of my tricks. This was, in fact, my usual lunch café, my usual sidewalk table, my device-inspired reservation, and she neither lived nor worked in that sector. This was, by all accounts, a coincidence, yes, a chance meeting. But now she has taken hold (again), taken residence in my mind and I fear I will not be able to bury it so easily this time…if I ever had.

Considering the scene I've painted and my seemingly wavering loyalties, you might ask me: can a man love two women at once? Is this natural? Does this happen often? Enlighten me, please! The answer is: they always do. They are in love with the woman they love and faintly in love with a "what-if." I'd be willing to wager women operate within a similar conundrum.

Running, the physical act of it, pumping knees and wobbly ankles, was never my strong suit. My body, even when I was younger, lean and flexible, simply wasn't designed for it. I was built low to the ground, engineered for the gentle, dignified motion of walking, a clean stride, perhaps even at a brisk pace, but not much more. Unsurprisingly, given my limitations, it took a few moments to catch up to her. There I was, out of breath and panting, bouncing in front of her, mouth half-open, almost dancing (and not dancing well), demanding her attention with all the grace and dignity of an open sore.

She looked at me with morbid curiosity, like I was the newly elevated village idiot. At first, I took her squinting eyes and distant posture as aloof and distracted, but, upon reflection, maybe it was paranoia. Despite my newly earned discomfort, perhaps it was she who was uncomfortable.

"Hey," I said. "Didn't you hear me calling you?"

She looked at me as if she felt she should know me but wasn't sure who I was. Her mauve eyes, distant and confused, were proving *me* to be the very mystery I so desperately wanted.

"No, I'm afraid I didn't hear you," she replied. "There was enough noise in the street to beat the band."

"Beat the band?"

"I'm sorry, are you not familiar with that phrase?" She asked as she crinkled up her nose and squinted. "I'll make a note of it."

I ignored her question. "I haven't seen you in a long time—how have you been?"

"Doing well. Learning."

"Learning?"

She seemed embarrassed by my questions or, at best, uninterested. She turned and continued down the sidewalk leaving me both alone and confused.

"Delius?" I said once, twice, three times.

Finally, she stopped and looked at me over her shoulder, her hair bouncing over her face before springing back.

"Sorry," she said with a dismissive grin usually reserved for cat-calling miscreants. "My name is Harriet."

Talis
(The Reds)

A few years ago, quite a few years ago now, Lark and I took a vacation to the Key Islands. We locked the house up tight, switched off the lights, and closed the heavy shades on the windows. There were still various light sources of varying intensities, hallway guiders and things of that nature, but overall, there was little light to be gathered by the sensors on the device. None of it was on purpose. Upon our return home, the device was groggy and slurring. Lark joked it had pried open the kitchen cabinet door and helped itself to our finest absinthe. The light was blinking green, yellow and red, like a maniacal traffic signal at an ancient intersection. It was both concerning and slightly sad to find the device in this state of distress. But what concerned me most, what frightened me to the very core, was the device kept settling on red.

It wasn't just me, Lark, too felt it—a rouge or malfunctioning device was dangerous and irresponsible. And, at times, it could be spiteful. Would it report us for neglect or incompetence? Would it claim the device at our vacation house had reported nefarious goings on during our vacation? Had it already done such things? Although the device was known to provide a generous leash, nearly to the point where you might even forget its omnipotent nature, it would pull you back by the scruff of the neck when you crossed an invisible and seemingly arbitrary line. Worst of all, information from the device was widely believed to weigh heavily on the ability to arrive. Fear it, I did.

The Grays were the first on scene—their nickname was derived from the gray uniforms and their typically dour personalities. They were considered the maintenance and troubleshooting team, but in reality they were a branch of the Intelligence Office. They poked and prodded the device with a delicate incompetence, like it was an angry, festering boil that might burst at any moment. They checked this and that, signal strength, solar sensitivity, etc. I'm really not sure what they did—each maneuver was performed with polite indifference, and their methods appeared haphazard and arbitrary. The entire production was rehearsed and vanilla, like they'd already been told, regardless of their findings, there was nothing wrong. Or there was something wrong and their findings were redundant. They compared data on their wristband devices and chuckled amongst themselves. It was a game, a little sport before lunch and their tummies were rumbling.

The Grays didn't ask questions—their shtick was exhaling in elongated, judgmental breaths and shaking their heads. Their reaction caused you to assume something was wrong, but you were never told directly about a problem, real or invented. They left with huff and a frown and announced, like disappointed parents presented with a dour report card, the Blues were on their way. They slammed the front door behind them without looking back.

The Blues appeared an hour later. They didn't attempt to hide the fact they were from the Intelligence Office. The Blues were known for the blue fabric covering they wore on their shoes when they entered a residence or office. The blue booties were meant to support the illusion they wanted a sterile, clean environment in which to work, but it was widely believed the booties were designed to collect traces of radiation and explosives as well as DNA of residents and visitors. The Blues were the talkers.

"Is there a reason you starved the device of light?"

"Were you aware the light sources were eliminated?"

"Did you attempt to open the device?"

"How long were you away?"

"Where did you go?"

"Why did you go there?"

"Can anyone vouch for you?

"Did you have permission?"

"Who else had access to your house?"

"What is your work office called?"

"Where is it located?"

"What days are you in office?"

"Your title?"

"Have you arrived?"

"Are you expecting to arrive?"

The Blues already knew the answers to the questions they were asking. We were aware they knew the answers, and they were aware that we knew they knew the answers. They didn't take notes. Much like those in many current professions, they were simply being kept busy. They exited with little fanfare other than an indignant turn of the lip and a quick wink of an eye on their way out.

Finally, the Reds.

The Reds were the ones you wanted to avoid. They were the ones you didn't want visiting. Although they all represented various elements of the Intelligence Office, the Grays and the Blues were buffoons—agents who didn't make the cut. Even in the moment I understood the irony, they weren't dissimilar to us and the others who hadn't arrived. The Reds, on the other hand, were hand-selected and deeply serious about their craft. Although completely dressed in black (when out in the field, at least), they were called Reds because it was the red light of the device that summoned them, that indicated they were on the way. The Grays were silent and gruff. The Blues were snarky. The Reds were dangerous.

The visits by the Grays and the Blues were civilized annoyances, ticking of boxes and signing of affidavits, like traveling clerks from the town office—expected and almost tolerable. But the Reds didn't knock—the door just opened and there they were. There were four of them: two serious looking hoodlums and two goons lugging red duffle-type bags.

Lark confronted them in the hallway.

"You can't barge in uninvited!"

"We can't?" The one with the dark eyes appeared to be in charge and was happy to respond, to scoff at the notion, his taunts honed over a hundred such visits, a hundred indignancies.

"No!"

"We just did."

"In this society, we have rights. We have freedoms!"

"What fool told you that?"

"What?"

"Who said you have rights? Who said you have freedoms?"

"No one needed to tell me!"

"You live by the grace and kindness of the device, nothing more."

Before he could protest further, Lark was thrown, face first, against the hallway wall and placed in hand restraints. Blood from a gash along his eyebrow left a trail of red along the white hallway paint before he was effortlessly tossed to the floor. Lark's additional questions and protests were quickly met with a mouth restraint. His continuing, mostly silent, protests were met with a black boot to the ribs and a long finger gestured toward him as a warning. The Red who'd thrown him against the wall, the one with the pointing finger, stood guard above him, his arms folded across his chest, his yellow eyes staring straight toward me.

Without awaiting instruction, I sat in a chair at the kitchen table. Though I assumed the kitchen table was a safe area, I was restrained to the chair by the scowling Red with eyes as black as night. He confirmed he was the one in charge when he stepped behind me to admire his accomplice's work. My heart rate was elevated and my breathing labored, but I was careful to not make any audible sounds or wiggle in the seat. When I looked up at the black-eyed beast, he glared through me like he was imagining my tomorrow and was certain I'd be displeased with it.

The two Reds with the duffle bags wheeled in a mysterious, silver cylinder about the size of large dog, some sort of mechanical detector. They used small, pink sponges to wipe areas of the floor, the walls, the doorknob, and Lark's forehead. Each sponge was fed into the wheeled cylinder for processing. When no alarm bells rang, they moved on to their next task. They emptied drawers and closets, tore covers off the bed and threw open any drapes they perceived to be overtly closed—perhaps a veiled message about showing deference to the device and its needs. They didn't appear to be looking for anything in particular or follow a pattern of organized inspection, but rather were intent creating chaos and on making a mess of things to teach us a lesson.

Once the drawers and cabinets were emptied, one of the goons asked the other to bring over the "sniffer." The wheeled cylinder was steered along the walls of the living room like they were taking Rover for a walk. Soon it beeped and began to glow a purplish-red, prompting the two handlers to dig into the red duffle bags and retrieve tools resembling a cross between an axe and crowbar. In an instant, and without much effort, they tore through a wall in the living room leaving a cavernous hole filled with myriad wires and insulation and an equal part dread. Lark moaned while I instinctively looked up at the Red in charge. He watched me out of the corner of his eye, but otherwise didn't react. I was too stunned and angry to cry.

Once the wall was open and its guts spilled into the center of the room like they'd dressed a kill in the field, the detector went silent and the glow softened. The goons looked at each other and shrugged. It appeared the damaging of the wall had at least temporarily satisfied the sniffer's fetish.

"False reading," said one of the demolition experts. He became sullen and disappointed, his shoulders slouched like a child who'd suddenly realized his birthday wasn't today but next month. Other than a snarled lip, there was little reaction from the Red in charge before the demolition team continued Rover's walk like nothing had transpired, like the wall's intestines weren't dumped in the middle of the rug. Lark again made a small sound, not much more than a whimper or light grunt of displeasure. He was met with another kick to the ribs by the sentinel with the crossed arms. His groan, the reaction to the cracked ribs, was allowed to pass. The Red leader shook his head at Lark, he was either displeased with his continued defiance or was wondering how such an idiot had survived this long. More than likely, it was both.

The demolition team was eyeing a second section of wall the sniffer flagged, it's satiated appetite obviously a temporary state. They nodded to each other with a glint of satisfaction, an "I love my job" type of wink and secret handshake that rabble reserves for these chummy moments.

The muscles of their necks were strained and stretched, ready to untwirl as they raised their axe-crowbars in response to the fuss from the sniffer as it worked itself into a beeping, glowing lather.

The Red misanthrope in charge was directly behind my chair. He stood so close I heard the air being pulled through his nostrils and caught the odor of his unholy breath as he exhaled (some sort of provolone). I also heard the clicking of the communicator in his ear. He raised a finger to the goons with the axes, the universal signal to pause, as he listened to whatever message was emanating from his handlers. I looked up over my shoulder, careful not to move too quickly or unexpectedly. His face, thus far a blank canvas, offered little emotion or, to be honest, humanity. It was a face that followed instructions to the letter, a brutally loyal face as likely to create as it was to destroy. His eyebrows slowly crunched together forming a single, dark brow, and his jaw became rigid—he was now visibly disturbed by whatever message he was receiving.

He held his right hand in the air, squeezed into a tight fist and the two demolition experts lowered the axes and, without visible distress or question, began to clear the flotsam and clean the various messes they'd created. The yellow-eyed sentinel pulled Lark to his feet with one meaty hand, released the restraints from his wrists and mouth and gently placed him in the chair across from me. Lark dizzily plopped into the chair, eyes wide and his head wobbly, loose upon his neck, but didn't say a word.

"Someone is looking out for you," black eyes growled,

the blackness squeezed into tiny, frowning crescents. "The walls will be repaired immediately and medical personnel will attend to his wound. Mention this to no one." Although his apology lacked a clear, discernable apology, I was reluctant to point it out.

It was the first and only time I'd seen the red light (and associated personnel) and I wasn't in a rush to relive the experience. As instructed, I told no one. Lark wholeheartedly agreed to the same. For many years after the incident, over decades of time passed, the questions remained: Who was looking out for us? And why?

Talis
(Camping)

Animals fought in the night, clawing and slashing, screaming, followed by a damp, metallic stench of fresh blood and salty urine. Wolverines, perhaps, raccoons or weasels, something with ample teeth and claws, bloodthirsty or protecting its young—my ears weren't trained to know the difference. The sounds filled the darkness, capsizing the quiet of night like a skiff caught on the swells of hurricane seas. There were screeches and moans, a low pitch gurgling growl and a kind of guttural clicking, perhaps a warning signal to those who would do harm. The scent of blood, though I couldn't see it, filled my nose as my imagination filled with fear and dread.

In the morning, when I told him (apparently, he'd slept through the entire affair), my father said it was a good omen, a welcome sign that life was returning to its normal state. Prey and predator in balance meant nature is balanced.

"Nature is spreading its wings, Talis," he said in that grateful, fatherly way with fluttering, butterfly fingers, like he'd been granted a reprieve from the lectern and nature was providing the morning's lesson. In the night, however, all that separated us from whatever death awaited was a trembling tent wall, a thin layer of membrane and woven fabric that I doubted would hold even a steady rain at bay. If these creatures of the night set their sights to us, considered us a threat (or dinner or both), I doubt they would have had much difficulty with either the pliable walls or the soft, pallid skin surrounding our throats.

The sounds ended as stealthily as they began. There was no elongated trailing off or boisterous carrying on, no apparent suffering, just sounds in full throat then nothing. How could such a paradox exist where the sound and smell of a violent act ends in a silence so full and present that one questions whether or not it ever was? Or was this simply the awaited relief, an exhale of knowing it wasn't us? No, not this time.

Sometimes I hear the sounds of that night, horrible and real, like the milk of a vibrant memory turned rancid. Sometimes when sleep eludes me, when I lay bathed in the yellow light of the device, my breathing slows and turns heavy before the blind sound of night specters terrifies me anew. Such is the depth and fullness of the memory. To this day, sleep remains an elusive gift.

The next morning, I desired to recreate the crime, perhaps to gain an understanding of what had transpired. Despite a thorough search, I found little evidence or remains of either the perpetrator or the victim. There was no tuft of matted and tugged hair or lost tooth wizened and loosened with age. I found no evidence of the battlefield. There was no rutted soil or trampled clump of forest grass. There was no obvious trench created by the victor dragging the carcass of the fallen to wherever such things are dragged and devoured. As designed and repeated ad infinitum, nature combined and blended the scene into the background and moved on.

Had I imagined the whole episode? Been bamboozled by the onset of a dream? No, it wasn't possible. I wandered in ever widening circles farther and farther from the campsite using a whittled tree branch, sharpened and hardened in the campfire, to poke and prod, to turn things over and inspect them. Other than my own weighty footsteps on decaying leaves and the snapping of twigs, all was quiet. Even blood's metallic scent, something I so distinctly remember, no longer hung in a cloud of the previous night. There was no indication a struggle had ever ensued. There was no one to blame.

⁓

When I was young, my father and I often camped in those same mountains my parents had driven to while celebrating their arrival. Rather than summon a transport, we'd dust off that same boxy convertible so the car, as my father put it, could "get some exercise." We took the long way, forsaking the polite, insistent voice of the guidance system in favor of memory and manual control, a slow, winding journey for those who weren't interested in getting somewhere quickly and had nothing but time. My father enjoyed a drive and sank deep into the seat, one arm extended forward with one hand on the steering wheel at either ten or two, maneuvering in slow, looping arcs like he was captaining a luxurious cruise ship. The jaunty hiss of rubber tires creating friction on the asphalt brought him particular joy.

"You hear that?" he'd ask above the unmistakable hum of rubber, his eyebrows high on his forehead, his lower lip quivering, ready to burst into a smile.

"Yeah," I'd answer without having to ask for clarification.

"Yeah," he'd say and turn his face toward me, a proud, red-lipped smile beaming across his face. He was never happier, his face never brighter than during our camping trips, lighter of being, almost free. But no one, not even my father, was truly free.

My father fancied himself an amateur survivalist. I remember printed paper maps and musty smelling books strewn across the backseat of the lumbering beast and a green mechanical compass with rounded edges and a black face curled into his dry, calloused hand. He certainly looked the part of someone who might disappear or blend into the mountains and fade away.

Regardless of season, it was always cooler in the mountains and we preferred to visit in autumn and winter when the sun settled in for more lengthy naps. When I close my eyes, I can see my father in heavy, olive-green wool pants with a million button-flapped pockets and a wool plaid shirt buttoned to his neck, a dark scarf tied in an unbalanced knot. As the weather grew colder, he added to the ensemble:

a cotton canvas barn coat or his grandfather's thick green and white wool sweater, at least a century old, fraying at the cuffs and collar and worn thin at the elbows. In the coldest months, a brown rabbit fur hat with long earflaps was perched atop his head and this, along with dark brown, oiled leather boots laced high on his shin, gave him the appearance of a rogue WWI pilot, long lost in time after an ill-fought dog-fight left him to parachute into enemy territory. I hear him clear his throat every minute like clockwork.

While in his camping uniform, he could easily be mistaken for a mountain hermit, though he was often clean-shaven and generally more sociable. But not always. The trips were his escape from the teeming masses of the city with both the noise and the expectations. He didn't like crowds, as they made him anxious and claustrophobic and in this, I was my father's daughter. He also didn't talk much about his work. He held several degrees in genetics (like everyone else), thirty years of college and a government job with a swollen pension due at an indeterminate time in an indeterminate future. He had an office or a lab that required most of his time, sometimes days, often nights, with work that left him exhausted and a bit crabby.

"I'm not important enough for anyone to care what I'm doing, but important enough to have to show up," he joked. Other than some vague allusions to unconnected professions, that was all I really knew.

The mountains were sparsely populated (perhaps not populated at all) even though the free-range lands were within a few hours transport to the north or west. I never saw other people: campers, hunters, hikers on a day trip. My father explained no one lived in these mountains even before the area was strip-mined, and for lack of a better description, left for dead. Every gram of mineral was extracted, washed, sieved, filtered, digested and the land pulverized, pulled inside out, left to gag on its own innards. The forest looked like someone had taken a sharpened garden spade and turned over every inch of soil, exposing the earth's soft, swollen belly. Anything of value, every tree, every blade of grass, was harvested bare. Now, seventy years later, the land was regenerating, trees and grass grew free, moving gracefully in a light breeze. Even fish, birds, and mammals returned in vast numbers.

But the land's renewal was tenuous. "If there's a need, the land will be stripped and processed again," he told me. "That's already been decided."

"People are afraid of ancient disease," he explained when I asked why there were no other campsites and no other campers. "That's why no one comes here. They're afraid disease hides in the soil, in the trees, in the animals, in the air. It's all lying dormant, waiting to be awakened, waiting for their turn."

I grew nervous and paranoid, like something was waiting for me behind each tree, under each rock, in the wind itself. "Is there disease?" I asked while turning my head from side to side, searching for tangible signs of the invisible. "Waiting in the mountains?"

He shrugged his shoulders and considered my question for a moment, looking pensive and calm, like he did when listening to the hum of the tires. "I don't know. Some disease is good. It lets air out of the balloon so it doesn't burst. Sometimes we're the disease, but not one of the good ones."

—

Most days I was a good listener. Or perhaps it was crippling shyness. But it was different in the mountains. I was different when the air was fresh, more curious and free-spirited, confident. I felt comfortable away from the city. This same fresh air, the purveyor of curiosity and confidence also arrived with a modicum of guilt. Was I breathing fresh air meant for someone more important or deserving? Had I stolen it, gulped it into my lungs and held my breath while the cashier was distracted? Plundered someone else's gold while they slept? Perhaps, I was an imposter in the mountains. But I wasn't the only one.

During one trip, I, again, found the courage to ask my father what he did for a living. When I'd asked him before, when I was younger, he'd provide disconnected bits and pieces: "Business," "Management," "Product Development," never anything concrete and never the same as the last time. For some reason, this time, he was more open to the discussion.

"I develop paints for electricity generation," he said. "We make the paint more efficient, increase its ability to recycle light into electricity. The latest paints can absorb any light source, natural or artificial, and they also absorb the carbon dioxide in the air which works essentially the same way. The paint on the outside of our house can harness enough energy each day to power the house ten-fold. The paint on the inside of the house recycles the artificial light almost 100%."

Despite his past tendency to avoid answering this particular question, he droned on and on. In a long-winded instant he provided a thousand data points, a hundred uses and a dozen things that made me wonder if he was being completely truthful. The words made sense, the numbers may even have added up, but his heart wasn't in it. He was going through the motions, like a disenchanted lover vociferously pledging his love to avoid an argument.

"What about transports? Is that how they're powered?"

"The paint on transports? Yes, the concept is the same."

Confident, "mountain me" called his bluff. "If your specialty is solar energy, why do you have a hydrogen vehicle?"

He laughed that booming, nervous laugh and itched his nose. "Seems strange, I know."

He tried to avoid the question, employing a warmer, steadier laugh to change the subject, a pivot to a more suitable topic. There he was, my father. I could see him now. This method had worked so many times in the past. He'd look past me, almost absentmindedly, like something far in the distance, or something in the depths of his mind, demanded his full and immediate attention. He'd crane his neck toward this phantom and clear his throat in the way all dads must, a quick, two-syllable "ah-hem" to throw me off the scent.

"That really isn't an answer," I persisted.

"You're not usually one to ask tough questions," he said and laughed again. "Do you really want the answer?"

"Of course!"

My confident father began to fidget, to twitch, utilizing two of the million pockets of his pants to calm his suddenly restless hands. For the first time in my memory, his mind failed in the search for the right words, leaving him unarmed and nude to the world. His eyes watered and he wiped them on his sleeve, pretending he was caught unaware by the season's non-existent allergies. His mouth hung open, searching for an elusive breath. His face, too, lost its perpetually confident shine and turned a dull gray, as if a hundred years of worry had raked down his cheek. If he didn't have his words, his perfect and timely and calming words, how could he wiggle out of a jam? In that moment, my father looked small, his shoulders slouched forward, his essence lured out of the brush and felled by a hunter hidden high in the trees. He aged twenty years in an instant. And when he finally spoke, I aged a little, too.

He didn't deliver the absurd and ridiculous joke I assumed was fermenting during the silence. In time, he found his words. "Rediscovered" may be a better description. They'd not abandoned him…at least not completely. His pensiveness was not without reason. He'd saved these very words for my ears, banked away where no one would look, like a paranoid pensioner stuffing the mattress full in preparation for a bleak and rainy day that may not arrive (or may not be recognized) before Death's boney knock. Yes, one day he knew these words would surface and he would need to surface them. He just didn't know they'd be said today. And they weren't what I expected.

The wind settled down for the evening and the leaves and needles of the trees were largely still. He looked up at them in the fading evening light, his neck sinewy and slightly reddened from scratching at invisible fleas, to see if the leaves might rattle once again, the gift of a tremble to provide him further cover. The trees offered no refuge as nature wants you bared to flesh, simple and instinctual, the way you were born into the world. And bare he was, his words the first crack in the ice before an unexpected and early melting of the lake cover. In time, all would collapse into the frigid water.

For many years after, I assumed his words, no doubt honed through practice and thought-through, were originally meant for Anna, tucked away somewhere safe on her benevolent behalf. After all, she was the one: angelic, chosen, the favorite, the one who'd arrived and gifted him a grandchild. Now I know they, the words that is, were actually meant for my heretical ears from the beginning. When he finally spoke them, it was with an amalgam of relief and embarrassment, like he'd unearthed the courage to admit to a crime after he'd been exonerated long ago.

He emitted a slow, steady exhale through the nose.

"Because I fear one day all will go dark and that blue beast will be the only light."

He scratched his neck again then continued, "Nature strives for balance. What comes next, for all of us, is an unfortunate result of Pride's failure."

"What comes next?" I asked.

He looked up toward the moon, it was hidden behind a thick layer of clouds that glowed along the edges.

"Madness."

It's easy to see now.

Lark
(What If?)

"Harriet?"

"Of course!" she replied quickly, though she didn't seem as sure as a moment ago. She placed her hands on her hips and closed one eye, measuring me up. "Should I know you?"

I didn't answer.

Delius (or Harriet) spoke differently than my Delius (or Harriet), being less direct and deliberate, more flowery and windy, like an old western movie burned slowly onto celluloid or an actress on stage playing a wallflower. Had it been that long since I'd seen her last? From my vantage point, she looked the same as I remembered, but her voice lacked a modern pace and tone.

Was this her new game—the stranger on the street—and I now merely a pawn, the sacrificial sort? Was it some new, rogue fetish for those who know those seedy pleasures of the flesh? Not that I was privy to the secret lives of others, to their needs, but it did seem out of character. Or was she so proficient and confident an actress to convince me she'd morphed into someone named Harriet? And what an odd, century-old name to now claim as her own.

"I've seen you around to be sure," she said and nodded with a growing degree of certainty. "I believe so, yes."

"Really, where?" I asked. The game continued unabated on the sidewalk near Café Drame, though I was unsure who was playing.

"Holtsford Park, if I'm not mistaken."

She was leaning away from me, a slight angle toward somewhere else, one leg ahead of the other like she was late for an appointment and each word spent on me was costing her money on the other end.

"That's odd. I don't think I've been to Holtsford in years," I said.

"Really? How strange that is to me," she said and tucked a tuft of curls behind one ear with her hand. She looked me up and down, focusing, momentarily, on the purple napkin still lodged in my collar. "You do look familiar."

I began to laugh.

"What's so amusing?" she asked after placing her hands high on her hips again.

"Are you done with this?"

"Am I done with what?"

"Your little game."

"I beg your pardon!"

She was committed, I'll give her that, trained in a thespian's high arts. It was so flawlessly engrained, it would require her to *act* if she wanted to appear unnatural.

"Fine. We'll do it your way," I said in a sort of exasperated mock surrender, throwing my arms in the air.

"Are you surrendering to me?"

"You mean metaphorically?" I asked.

"No."

"Then, no!"

"Don't flip your lid!"

"What?"

"I'll ask again: Are you surrendering to me?"

"What? No."

With this surreal interaction, I began to sense this was, in fact, someone named Harriet or at least someone that was not Delius. She was just different enough to be different and just strange enough to be a stranger. I considered again: was she a master thespian (sans stage costume) at the peak of her craft? Or was I some unsuspecting rat being led around a clandestine maze awaiting my comeuppance of poisoned cheese and a dissected brain?

As it turned out, when presented with the opportunity, enticed with something shiny and new, I chose adventure and curiosity. The danger of those magical mauve eyes lured me in despite the strong likelihood the cheese was laced with cyanide. Yes, I decided on the spot, this was a game I wanted to play. It would be a little sport, a fling, a lark (Ha!) nothing more. She'd piqued my interest and I would see this through. Perhaps that was her goal. Sly girl.

After a few more awkward moments of fumbling banter, I asked for her device code. She didn't refuse, but she didn't agree. Instead, she turned the gesture on its head, a bamboozlement, and asked for mine. I gave her my office device code. Fools, especially sly fools, need not always be so reckless.

I walked back to my lunch table, chest inflated like an ornately feathered fowl, shoulders thrown back. Was there even a small hop in my step? I must have been a sight to my fellow diners, this lurid, strutting peacock who, only a few minutes prior, sputtered and choked, tripped over his own feet while attempting to gain a woman's audience. Now, I glided along the sidewalk carefree and bold, even daring to step on the cracks and crevices in the cement without fear of breaking anyone's back. By the time I reached the table, my head was throbbing and I needed water. All this walking did not agree with me. Ego, it appears, can mask both warning signs and common sense, smother them, snuff them out like a burning candlewick exposed to a gale wind. Still, I didn't care. I was in the midst of a "what-if."

I felt a little…what was it? Proud? Yes, I felt proud. I was keen on tricking myself into thinking maybe I deserved this wayward dalliance, but in a good way like when you win something in a raffle you shouldn't have entered or collect a reward even though you know full well it will lead to ruin.

For those looking to cast judgment, to point fingers and yell from your comfortable, fluffy clouds in full-throated sanctimony —you must wait. You must hear me out, at least a little longer. My intention was not to harm or deceive Talis. Selfish, yes, but not meant to deceive. The harm, the deception, had already been cast—we'd harmed each other already, though not with conscious intent. Our station in life had harmed us. The act of togetherness and our joining each other was our undoing. We, us, are a failed experiment, an almost, a "just missed" awarded a dreaded second place while violently shoved down to the lower pedestal. We are the yellow light that emanates from the device and shines its futile warmth into every crevice, every nook and lands upon our wrinkled, exposed skin and curved spines, our shrunken souls. Yes, all that. We're a failed family and there's no hiding from it. Yet, life must go on for we are not in control of its end point. We're all a moon colony away from realizing our greatest dreams, our long awaiting adventure or ushering in our untimely demise. At least Lazarus had his time.

What was I missing? I was not part of Team Delius or, more accurately, *a* Team Delius. I was not a partner in a partnership blessed and bestowed with arrival. No, I have no purpose. I suspect Talis would say the same. Now it was time to live.

Now you may judge. Feel free. Go ahead if you must. I will sleep tonight regardless. My unearned arrogance is on display for all to see, my next feathery saunter back to the lunch table. For tonight or tomorrow may be my last tonight or tomorrow. We all know this is true.

And where did I still fit into all of this…future? To me, the future is not so very much what is to come (though I can see the argument should that be your view), but who will be there. Things that are to happen are in no small part a function of those who are present when they do happen. If I'm not there, the things I may have done will not be done—and therefore do not need to be undone or as likely, apologized for. And since I am not destined to arrive, I need not worry about my progeny screwing things up for everyone else. It's a sort of "get out of guilt" card for us perpetual second-placers. The future, it turns out (unsurprisingly) is reserved for the winners.

———

There were fights, of course. There always are. Talis holds the peculiar belief that a fight, a solid, old-fashioned brawl ("spit and piss" she elegantly calls it) is an indicator of passion in a relationship. She insists a good go-around is required to achieve a healthy rebalancing and find a hard reset. She often dove in, head, feet and arms first, whirling about, flailing her hands, voice elevated, driving home some nonsensical angle she'd concocted. The win too, was paramount. There had to be a clear winner and that winner would not be me. For if, by some stroke of luck or unexpected turn, I could claim to be the victor, to raise my arms in the tradition of a champion, it was with full knowledge there would be, by decree, a rematch and perhaps a second rematch, a cycle which would continue until things were made right.

In the pitch of battle, she was darkly deranged, like she'd discovered someone had snuck into her closet in the middle of the night and sawed the heels from her favorite shoes. I was a little afraid of her. Seething passion boiled to the surface and heated her cheeks and dilated her pupils so wide they could swallow you whole. Anna knows this all too well.

I doubt it would displease Talis to know that little secret.

Of course, I never saw the value in her all or nothing approach. I'm a picker of battles—not a hair trigger that litigates every lessor slight as if my family honor has been savaged and slapped across the face with a crisp, white leather dueling glove. I fight when a fight is necessary and meaningful and where an end is essential, not because it's there and not because I'm looking to conjure some emotion from thin air. Fighting, to me, is not an act of passion, but rather an act of betrayal, a summoning up of all that's wrong, not a search for what's still right. We clearly don't see eye to eye. Stylistically we're incompatible, like the name of an old English pub. That's become clear. If only we knew earlier. The Birth Office knew. As did Anna.

—

Why was I was spared from the moon tragedy? If I was to be the last of my kind, the last of my family, the end of the family line, then what would be the use? What would be the reason for not being there when it all went wrong? If there was ever someone who was expendable, someone that would not be missed, certainly that was me. The civil servant conducting the interviews looked at me like I was the type. When he saw me, his bushy eyebrows bounced toward the heavens in a kind of "what do we have here?" As he flitted through my tidy file projected on the device, his hands were raised in a gesture of prayer and he was making little popping sounds with his tongue while emitting low hums of satisfaction. He leaned back into his chair then exhaled a whistle out through the nose and crossed his arms. He seemed satisfied, like he'd finally found a key he was hunting for after remembering to check the obvious kitchen drawer. I thought he'd sign me up on the spot, have me shaved, uniformed, and rocketed by day's end.

Yet something saved me. A mistyped description perhaps or a box missing a critical checkmark. Maybe deep in the file was a report from a grammar school principal saying I lacked sophistication or demonstrated questionable reliability or despite innumerable opportunities, I just couldn't color within the lines. The device, if nothing else, possessed all the information. It held all the dirty details and all our perceived greatness, all the honors and demerits, all the secrets. At least, that's what we were taught: fear the device. Love the device. In the end, it made no difference for me.

Of course, this wasn't something I knew at the time, I was blind to the subtle dissembling that grew and festered in a parallel timeline. I assumed my life was in front of me. I thought generations of pointy nosed carbon copies would follow in lock step, mediocre grades and a sallow disposition. We were taught in school, encouraged in college, that we were the best of us. We were the best society had to offer and, one day, without fail, the device would emit a telling and delicious green that filled the room with a luminous clover-colored hue blessing us with our arrival. Our partners, our wives and husbands, would be overjoyed knowing all their decisions, including our courtship, had paid full and generous dividends. Our parents too, would be beside themselves with giddiness and grandchild-inspired pride, their nicknames, in due course, inscribed on a ceramic mug or plucky t-shirt preceded by the words "World's Greatest." Yes, these were the promises made to us. These were the deceptions. But one was always in too deep to change course should the winds fail or the seas become ornery. You were limited to a single course of action and the device, its emotionless algorithm always at the ready, is uncompromising.

The thing is, all of life had the feeling of being preordained. Work, the work of human beings, the imperfection of making our way through it all, had been reduced. There were no rock-bottoming failures and no stars who shone above all others. Technology and medical advances had mitigated many of the dangers our ancestors faced, but along the way, sanitized the experiences of life. Our collective existential path was forced into one viable outcome. This flatness of mind and body had become so pervasive and safe there was only one goal that possessed any meaning: procreation. The one failure we feared was also the one reason for living. We, us, all of us, have allowed our lives to whittle down to one sharpened point of the stick. That, I'm afraid, is what humans do when they've already accounted for their physical needs. Our safety and our prosperity are also our most destructive forces.

Was there really someone or something high up somewhere making these decisions, or was it fate? I have my suspicions. I do know the decision wasn't mine to make. I would not have allowed Talis to spend her evenings sunk deep into our marriage bed, curled and contorted, her face heated and swollen, no longer possessing the energy to hide her tears. Why would society rob this fine woman of her one desire? Why would we deny her the one blessing that would give her control over her own humanity? And worse, this is all because of my lack of fitness. These are questions I can now pose, now that the hope we'd nurtured and fed and kept alive in our hearts has torn and faded before blowing away with the evening wind.

Am I just trying to justify everything I've done, all my feelings and all my actions? That's likely, but I have to work through it. I have to find my beginning and the middle or I risk not recognizing the end.

—

Was I expecting marriage to be perfect? No. And yes. We all imagine the future perfection of our existence. We envision the soft landing once the die is cast and the decisions are made, when we wipe the sleep from our eyes and our person, the one we're destined to have at our side becomes clear. If we don't aim for perfection, even expect it, why would we commit ourselves to any endeavor? Why would we risk traversing a snowy, winding road along a narrow cliff's edge knowing the final stop would fail to meet expectations? But no, I didn't expect our union to be perfection. I did, however, expect all we had accomplished, together and individually, to lead to our arrival. And for the middle class, the Mid-Levs, leaving another generation to take a swing at perfection was as close to perfection as could be expected.

Life has taught me things change and, more importantly, people change. Talis changed. I changed. Reflecting back, there were little, perhaps trivial hints of things to come like in the aftermath of Talis assembling a peanut butter sandwich. So simple an act it appeared at first glance. Yet the jar of peanut butter itself looked like the scene of a particularly gristly murder, swirls of purple jelly polluting the sandy brown, and deep, unapologetic puncture wounds from a knife wielded like an ice pick. This subtle act of violence was so telling, like she'd been searching for an outlet, a vessel to fill with her pain, and found one in the most innocuous place: lunch. Still, it was far better a place to aim her displeasure than the flattish side of my skull or the soft, fatty trench between my shoulder blades as I turned my back toward her. Many of the clues, though, were so subtle they escaped my notice and even now remain lost to time.

Near the end, there I was, the mutilated remains of peanut butter left in the jar to rot or at the very least, sealed away to bleed from the inside out. Once I came to grips with this, all of it, the pain began to subside. I'm sure when she penned her list of my ruddy faults, it was much bolder and relevant then any I've endeavored to concoct. I don't believe we were a poor fit or loveless or lacked in friendship. Our physical characteristics were, if nothing else, reasonable and acceptable. Mediocrity, we're led to believe, is not akin to a death sentence.

Our behavior? We towed society's line, functioned within the confines of our station, at times more so. We gave little reason for the device to assign us demerits or, perish the thought, be assigned for a meted, red-light punishment or banished for an undefined term to an undisclosed location. Someone or something somewhere obviously drew different conclusions. The running down of a list, I'm ashamed to say, solidifies me as an observer rather than a doer, one in possession of a gregarious canine without being its master.

What does all this mean? What am I attempting to say? There comes a time to give up the pursuit, to accept and to pivot toward something else, something attainable, even something that might make you happy. Accepting failure is not a failure itself, but rather a wake-up call and a point in which to create a break in time.

Talis
(The Scar)

I remember Anna's screams.

And the blood.

So much blood. It was like a sheep I'd been counting in the night had returned to haunt me, slit open by an unseen hand to douse me in its warm, greasy innards. There it was, a jagged slash down Anna's forehead, her brow sliced clean open, blinding her in one eye with the salt of her own blood. I peered into the depths of her skull, studied it, whitish bone and pink flesh sawed through. Yes, I'd tried to saw through her. It was me. I was the violence, and the violence was me.

Anna's voice competed with the voice in my head, each fighting to be heard, attempting to outduel the other. Which one was it though? Which voice led me to raise a blade to another. What specter led me to butcher my own sister? Despite my hope of blaming some inner demon who'd coaxed me down a path of violence, pulled the marionette strings taut and controlled my actions, there was only one true voice. There was always one voice and it was my own.

There it was again, that metallic scent of fresh blood. I'd missed it terribly. I pulled in a long breath through the nose, savoring the sweet taste it left in my mouth. Was the call of the carnivore soothing or was it nature's signal to stop, an indication the job was done?

My ears were ringing, drowning out Anna's words. Her question remained unintelligible and shrill, floating about the room without taking form. When my mind settled, became quiet, more malleable, I heard her voice, tiny and far away.

She was asking "Why?"

A good, fine and sensible question. I didn't provide an answer. The serrated camping knife, honed sharp by my own hand under my father's unknowing guidance, was held firm in my white-knuckled fist. Blood ran down my hand and wrist, dripping, pooling on the floor near my feet. There was more on the walls, and the ceiling, happy pink dots and somber red droplets. In an instant, it was everywhere. Consuming everything.

"Why?"

How dare she ask! We both knew why. But I wasn't going to say it. I would not be the one to say it. I couldn't look at her, the disfigured girl who would not laugh again for ten years. I turned away from her and her cries for help.

"You don't know what it's like," Anna whispered as she curled her body tightly on the floor. "You don't know what it's like to give one up."

"I don't care!" I hissed. And I didn't.

—

Anna never told anyone about that day. Outside of our immediate family no one knew how she received the injury. They didn't need to ask. Everyone assumed correctly: my parents, the doctor, the rotating turnstile of haughty plastic surgeons. All of them. I spent a month in isolation as agreed. My recovery plan they called it, my chance to heal. My chance to heal! No, I would never heal and now Anna would never forget. That, of course, was the point.

Sometimes, I still hear Anna's screams like the animals in the night. I awaken to them, surrounding me, echoing through the room, not ceasing even though I'm conscious and far from sleep. I never expected them to go away, but I assumed they would fade over time. Time's slog, of course, has helped. It always does just like they tell us.

In time, we became friends again, Anna and I, sharing bits of our lives with each other, softening what I'd done to her. We sometimes even talk about her daughter, my niece, Lotti. The conversations are superficial and forced, but polite. They're also never about Lazarus. And to be clear, Anna is not at fault. She did not willfully elbow herself to the front of the line at my expense. Her intent was not to diminish me. She simply accomplished what I had hoped for myself. What I had dreamed for myself. And because she did, I have not. All that remains for me is a dream. She hasn't told me she forgives me, and I don't believe she will. I don't really forgive her, either.

It may be that Anna wears this unusual scar as a badge of honor. I've heard Echoes carry many scars either from battles or accidents or the cold steel of meted discipline. However, it's unusual for commoners to be disfigured in such a way or in any way, really. In this sense, I've made Anna special. I've made her unique. What an odd thought. What was meant as punishment by an unhinged and jealous sister (yes, I know this), a violent and selfish act to be sure, has become what many consider an attractive trait. My attempt to degrade her has made her better. How sad this is for me.

I have so much anger yet lack the strength to release it productively. When medicine was in its infancy, they said physical exercise, the strain and sweat of movement, and a quickening of the heart was a good release of anger and anxiety. Of course, that's been disproven a hundred times over. I've tried ancient meditation, twisting my body into an impossible pretzel until my spine cracked and muscles tore from the bone.

The alleged calming effects of music, slow tempos and sounds of nature were put through their useless paces. I've even tried, I'm embarrassed to admit, the purposeful hurting of myself. I would fling my body against a sturdy wall after a running start or send myself tumbling down a flight of stairs, bouncing about and cracking my skull. I was often left bloodied and sore. None of it provided any relief. None would soothe me for more than a fleeting moment. I carry a gritty, irreconcilable anger. I understand this now. And Lark has borne the brunt of it. He's been the unwitting target of the lashing out and the lectures, the contempt and the sneers of disappointment. My rudderless partner is not fully deserving of all of it, but I expect he'll be on the receiving end of my venom, one way or another, until the day we expire.

Lark
(On Lazarus)

In my heart, I believe Talis coveted Lazarus much like she covets many aspects of Anna's life. A taboo subject to be sure and one I never dared raise in her presence (I mentioned earlier I'm a coward). The lives of the two sisters were never in direct competition, but the comparisons, in Talis' mind, were both stark and omnipresent. The tension (there was always tension between the sisters) came mostly from Talis. I don't believe Anna gave it much thought. That's the tendency of older siblings, though she possesses a gruesome scar as a daily reminder and earned the right to be bitter if she chose.

I only knew Lazarus for a short time (he was already assigned to Pride when I met Talis) but was well acquainted with the legends and the stories and the innuendos. It was, however, easy to see his memory was more complicated than his life, as the legends and stories and innuendos were generally uninspired. Talis believed that Anna believed he had served his purpose, proved most useful, successfully achieving an arrival before Anna rocketed him off to Pride—to his doom—with barely a running the dock "bon voyage" or waving of a tear-stained handkerchief. When his expiration date came due, he was alone, serving another equally critical purpose in the way we all secretly hope to pass.

As they both knew Lazarus, he was their loss. For both of them. But Talis suffered more because she wanted to be the one suffering more. She searched it out with a bloodhound's tenacity and gripped it with cracked, dry fingers until they bled. And Anna was busy preparing for a child.

"We make sacrifices," Talis' father said after Pride—and Lazarus—were lost. His voice was calm and slow of pace… the kind reserved for bomb squad leaders and rakish politicians. "We all make sacrifices." Anna understood. Talis did not. Lazarus, as far as I knew, was indifferent.

Yes, I find myself in a sour mood. These thoughts, these memories still churn in my stomach and are difficult to reconcile. I carry too much disappointment to be reliably neutral.

***

Anna selected green eyes and brown hair and olive skin for her daughter. "If the hair curls, so be it," she said with a laugh. "I'll leave a few surprises. I love surprises!"

Anna gave birth to Lotti and her twin a month after the failure of Pride. Lotti's twin was Anna's second sacrifice in as many months—a dowry.

But Anna was not as unscathed as she appeared. Instead,

she focused her energy on preparation, a plan, another ruse.

"I named her Lotti so they can never find her," Anna confided to me in a silky whisper after too many glasses of warm absinthe. I remember those words in my ear as she listed toward me, barely in her chair, her warm, moist breath on my cheek. Until I met Harriet with her peculiar, antique name, I didn't understand what Anna meant. Harriet explained it to me. All of it. She told me what Pride was and what it wasn't. And she told me what was coming. Anna, unsurprisingly, was ahead of her time.

Whoever might look for Lotti, they never found her. She was ushered off to boarding school at an early age and rarely visited home and never for very long. That's how I remember her, in her smart boarding school uniform, white with green and blue plaid and heeled shoes that clicked when she walked. I always heard her coming down the hall, clicking, but when she left, she vanished without a sound. There were never photographs or holograms taken, and I don't remember ever seeing one of Lotti. I doubt they exist.

To an outsider, Lotti might seem the daughter Anna never wanted, shunned and shoved into different corners of the room like the embarrassing, belching uncle you're obligated to invite to a holiday, but nothing was further from the truth. She was being protected, wrapped in moving blankets and armor, placed in a box stored on a lonely attic shelf, gathering dust and slowly fading from memory. Even Anna herself, when asked, had difficulty recalling Lotti's features: her eyes, her skin, and her hair. Like Pride, it was all a mirage.

Talis
(Ghosts in the Night)

We had a favorite camping spot. It was a small clearing surrounded by birch and pine trees not far from a narrow walking path. The ground was slightly higher than the surrounding area, so the patch of dirt and grass remained dry and firm year-round. We gathered fallen wood and stray branches, set a mosquito barrier, and made a campfire. If I was sullen or moving too slowly for my father's taste, he'd make a game of it, seeing who could gather the most wood in five minutes or who could find and identify the most edible mushrooms. I always won. He always let me win.

Down a slight hill but within sight of camp, a gurgling river flowed with mostly shallow, fast-moving water. Over several visits we created pools of slower moving water by stacking rocks into semi-circles to the side of the main current. We used small saws and my hunting knife to cut lengths of tree branch and lay them across the pools, balanced on the rocks. Then we strung fishing lines around the branches every two or three feet. My father was very specific in his instructions: form a loop with the line then thread it through the eye of the hook before weaving the hook back through the loop and pulling the line tight. He made me practice securing the hooks on many occasions before it became primarily my job. Once the lines were ready, we dug earthworms and grubs for bait. I always felt sorry for the worms, their clammy lengths flailing about blindly, curling back against themselves before being skewered on metal talons and drowned in cold water. We returned a few hours later to collect our catch: trout and an occasional crawfish. I was very proud.

When the sun was strong, we began the campfire using a magnifying glass and birch bark then kept it burning day and night. Initially, my job was to collect the birch bark and miscellaneous twigs and small sticks. I used the well-honed camping knife, two sizes too big for my hand, to slice long, thin strips of bark from the birch trees then rolled the strips and stuffed them into my coat pocket. To make the fire, we surrounded the strips of birch with twigs, dry leaves, and grass then used the magnifying glass to aim the concentrated sunbeam onto an edge of the bark. Over time, this also became one of my tasks.

A few years earlier, we moved large rocks up from the river and created a circular fire pit. At the time, some of the rocks were bigger than I was, and instead of trying to lift them, I rolled the unbalanced beasts as best I could, nearly falling over myself as I pushed with all my might. The effort left the knees of my pants torn and soiled black and my fingertips reddened and tender with dirt permanently trapped under my fingernails. But it was worth it.

In the fall, we set wire snare traps for rabbits and the occasional squirrel or raccoon. Cleaning mammals was much more delicate and difficult than cleaning the fish and oddly emotional. Cleaning a rabbit felt like I was slicing open one of my childhood teddy bears and pulling out the stuffing, though the texture and smells were infinitely more unpleasant. We dried and salted the skins and sewed them into functioning, though ill-conceived hats (my father's favorite rabbit hat was made by more seasoned hands). When we had enough square footage, we sewed the skins into a blanket. I may still have one of the blankets, like a memory, tucked into a dusty corner of a forgotten storage space.

On more than one occasion, as a fresh rabbit cooked on a spit over a mature fire (and looking nothing like a beloved stuffed animal), my father would point upward toward the sky and tell me how people thought the moon was made of cheese. He must have told me the story a hundred times but I'd laugh no matter how many times I'd heard it. Then he'd laugh and give me a bear hug, the coarse wool of his shirt scratching the skin on my face, making it red and pimply. As soon as he noticed the reaction to the rough wool on my skin, he'd rub my face with his hand until it calmed. "Sorry, sorry!" he'd say in quick succession. I didn't mind.

These trips are where I began to appreciate the stars and, of course, the moon. My father, unsurprisingly, was also a dreamer. On one trip when I was older, he seemed particularly philosophical and while poking the fire with a long stick, took a drink from a flask of his homemade whiskey (he called it "moonshine" with a laugh because, according to him, it made you dream at night). It's difficult to know what made him think about the future (I mean, we all do) or specifically the future without him.

"I want you to teach everything you learn here to your child," he said. "Pass all of the knowledge along." Then he added with a shrug of his shoulders, "In case I'm not here."

"Have I been paying enough attention?" I asked, doing my best to ignore his last comment.

"Only you can answer that question," he said and passed the flask over to me. "Do you feel like you've been paying attention?"

"No," I said. I was being honest. His head and neck were craned toward the stars and he continued to stare upward, silent.

The thought of having a child of my own hadn't crossed my mind at that age, but from that point I was an eager, if flawed, student.

On one trip, my father brought a large, air-tight chest made of resin. The monstrosity filled the entire back seat of the blue beast and as we drove, I felt it behind me, watching, observing, judging like a second parent.

We filled the chest with fishing line and hooks, two knives and a sharpening stone, a magnifying glass, a compass, a portable water purifier, a first aid kit, two blankets with sleeping pads, a small tent, a solar lamp, a bow with a dozen arrows for hunting deer and other miscellaneous items like the meals astronauts eat. Lastly, he put in two green, rubbery suits, a twentieth century rifle, and a gross of bullets.

We buried the chest twenty paces to the north of our campsite, between two birch trees. My father carved an "x" into the bark of the tree on the left and a "y" into the tree on the right. "In case we forget anything, we have access to supplies," he said and winked. "'X 'comes first, so if you find the 'X', it's buried to the right, if you find the 'Y', it's buried to the left."

My father kept a rusty, thick handled shovel in the truck of the car like someone out of a 20th century mobster film. I imagined it being wielded by a drab but menacing figure with a high forehead mostly covered by a bowler hat who spoke in short, grunting phrases. One day we dug up the chest of supplies because we forgot something or other— likely on purpose. It was a filthy, exhausting process akin to exhuming a body from its resting place. Every opportunity was a lesson. Every moment was an opportunity.

On more than a few occasions, I had the bad luck of contracting poison ivy. In the past, a vaccine was adminis- tered, largely mitigating the shiny three-leafed monster, but now, since few, if anyone, ventured outside the cities, the vaccine had gone out of style and there were no longer stores of it waiting to pierce our flesh.

I soon learned I was highly allergic to poison ivy.

My eyes swelled like I'd been grossly overmatched in a

boxing ring and red, itchy bumps formed along my skin. The worst were the soft, warm spaces behind my knees and the bony parts of my ankles—the areas where there was no membrane covering my skin. These two baleful places itched incessantly and my jagged fingernails dug deep crop rows in my skin and even drew blood. It was difficult to hide my discomfort.

I wasn't allowed to discuss our trips to the mountains, and my father, when he saw me itch and heard the unmistakable sound of nails scraping on skin, was quick to remind me my silence was best. Attending classes a few days after exposure was unbearable, akin to sequestering a severe bout of hiccups in the quiet section of a library. It took every ounce of concentration and discipline to remain still and appear carefree and allow the itch to fester and run its cruel course, eventually, resolving itself.

The school pods were equipped to detect attention patterns, sending detailed pulse and temperature information to the instructor to weed out those who were daydreaming or, in my case, squirming and contorting their body in mute combat. Often, my parents received a message on the device informing them of my tendency to act out and disrupt. This news, of course, was met with my father's nervous laugh. At times it was difficult for me to know the difference between the humorous and the problematic.

It was during these camping trips that I also discovered my irrational fear of wasps. Of course, what was real to me was labeled irrational by others. One summer I was gathering blueberries, placing them into a small wicker basket and covering them with a rectangular piece of fabric. I was squatting low, crouching down on my knees to reach berries deep in a bush. Then I heard them. All of them with their high-pitched hum and battle-ready drumming. I'd set a foot on the entry to a nest, my body twisting, my shoe grinding down their earthen entryway like an ancient movie monster destroying a city gate. They were upon me in an instant. The black and yellow devils were angry and determined, and they did not discern accidents or ignorance from threats. It didn't matter to them.

The basket flew skyward and the blueberries scattered in a thousand directions. I ran faster than I thought I could run down the worn path, gliding over swollen tree roots and jagged rocks, my heart pumping, back to the campsite. By some miracle, I lost them, impaled by only a single sting resulting in a festering red lump pulsating on my right shoulder. My father placed an antiseptic pad on the sting after inspecting with his finger, poking and squeezing until I winced. Then he laughed.

"They usually won't bother you unless you bother them."

"I think I did bother them," I said.

"Then you were lucky you only got one!" he said and laughed again.

Even when one escapes from certain danger relatively unscathed, there is still a price to be paid. To this day, I still freeze at the sight of a wasp, buzzing its fearsome buzz, hoping beyond hope that it won't notice me, and me, oblivious to the fact that I'm not to be noticed.

There was something else about the mountains.

There were noises and strange things and animals and blood. Rivers that gurgled and fish that frolicked. Wasps that sting and ivy that poisons. I've mentioned these. But there were also people. Not our people, not the ones who inhabited the city and were seeking an escape for their mind and an escape for their body. The mountain people were the ones who disappeared from society and never returned. Now, you must understand, I never saw them. Or heard them. Or even found traces they existed.

They were ghosts in the night.

Or maybe they were simply a legend, the product of religious mitigation and the adaptation of modern sensibilities. It's likely they didn't exist at all except to populate the human mind and its insatiable need for "what ifs." After all, if we can dream of the distant moon, it makes full sense we can dream of the mountains on our own horizon.

"Talis," my father said late one night in a more serious tone than I expected. My face was kissed by the light and warmth of the campfire, while a few feet away his face hid in shadow and smoke. He pointed a muscular arm toward the night sky, but rather than a light-hearted moon of cheese, his subject was something new and unexpected.

"See that reddish one there?"

"I think so, there's so many," I answered, trying to follow his finger, attempting to discern his subject hanging amongst the thousands of glowing dots.

"That one there, that's Mars. That's the future. Someday soon we'll live there," he said. My father, the dreamer.

But he was wrong.

—

A wooden light post marked the narrow road to our camp. The bluish light perched on top provided a beacon to guide us, an indication to turn onto the first unpaved paths that led to our hidden campsite. My father used to joke that one day his recycled body would be used to light that beacon and to guide me on my future journeys, but even at a young age I knew it was powered by carbon dioxide and sunlight—not carbon.

One trip he brought the hulking convertible to a squealing, stammering stop, the rubber tires melting from the friction, the unmistakable acidic odor bathing us in an unpleasant cloud. He stared straight ahead silently and drummed his fingers on the steering wheel. It was near twilight and the beacon was just beginning to flicker, coming to life in the approaching darkness.

"Is this our turn?" he asked still staring forward. Rather than his usual casualness, both hands were squeezed tightly around the steering wheel and his knuckles were drained white. "Or should I keep driving?"

I looked up from the passenger's seat at the light post, then upward higher toward the beacon. I'd never paid much attention during the drive, so I couldn't be certain.

"I think so," I said.

"Should I turn here?"

"Yes," I said with as much confidence as I could muster while refusing to look toward him.

"Here?" he asked again, his eyebrows raised high up on his forehead. "You sure about that?"

"Yes," I repeated.

A cold, disappointed "Hmmmmmm…" fell from his lips as he put the car back into gear and continued straight up the original road. I sat low in my seat, quiet, defeated, though I wanted to release the restraints and crawl under the seat.

After a few seconds, he slowed the car and made a great, looping turn to reverse direction and turned onto the dirt road at the beacon and let fly a hearty laugh.

Lark
(Harriet's Back)

Harriet's back was pitted and scarred like farm-worked land, and her skin was discolored with bruises of blue and green and red. Even Anna's scar was mild in comparison. The damage to her back, whatever the cause, resulted in reptilian ridges and indentations and shallow trenches that spanned almost the full length of her torso. When I asked, she allowed my hands to run along the surface. There were dips and bumps, small edges formed on the skin and in the ravaged muscle underneath. I couldn't fathom what had caused this trauma, these inhumane and obvious injuries. I'd never seen (or felt) anything like it. When I closed my eyes and used my hands as a guide, it was worse. There were both crests of hardened callus and soft pools of hidden liquid that shifted and altered shape under my palms. It held a life of its own, like a chrysalis about to split and empty its emerging kin.

At first it was such an odd sensation to run my hands over Harriet—it was…different. Talis' back, for example, was a soft and delicate place, smooth, pleasant with muscles fitted with the skill of a master craftsman and hung in place with hooks of due care. There were no surprises, no deviations, and when your hands wandered, everything was where you'd expect, intact and purposeful…elegant. My hands, not my eyes, told me Talis' back was perfect.

I grew to recognize each of Harriet's ridges, each shallow, each imperfection mapped by my hands and etched into my mind. Even in the pitch of night I knew exactly where I was. For example: her right shoulder, almost at the rounded peak, held a shallow crater about an inch in diameter and a quarter of an inch deep. It was concave like someone had taken a small ice cream scoop and dug out a hollow of skin and muscle. Down low on her right side, in the center near her spine, were four small bumps of scar tissue running upward from the top of her buttocks. The third bump was slightly elongated so the four bumps formed the Morse Code letter F: dot, dot, dash, dot. In time, I even grew to care for her scars. What an odd thing to say, even stranger to think, but yes, these scars made her attractive to me. She was different and undeniably a new discovery. She was a new type of perfection, but there were costs.

Often Harriet was in pain from these injuries. Though she never outwardly complained, small jolts of discomfort contorted the muscles of her face. When we were alone, I massaged her back, attempting to break down the scar tissue by rubbing with my thumb and index finger and the firm palm of my hand. It did little to ease her suffering, but I tried. In a cavalier moment, I asked what happened, what caused these wounds. Clearly, they were not the result of a single accident or event, but a pattern of something more sinister. But she didn't trust me enough to part with her secrets—at least not yet. It wouldn't be the last time I asked.

"We're not all as lucky as you," she laughed one day in response to my question. It was her only response to the question other than a gritty silence she'd mastered. I believe she felt pity for me and my weaknesses whenever I attempted to project pity upon her.

To my touch, especially to her disfigured back, Harriet elicited soft grunts and groans, little tremors and breathy sighs. I couldn't tell whether they were sounds of satisfaction or pain, or whether my touch elicited a modicum of pleasure or added to her perpetual discomfort. Perhaps it was somewhere in between. In these moments, I was stricken with a curious blindness, robbed of my own tepid ability to discern another's pleasure from their pain, light from darkness, maybe even good from evil.

One night in a fit of rage and half lost in a dream, she took my sallow neck in her hands and squeezed. Life drained from me in truncated puffs of air, my narrow, soft neck no match for her skilled hands. My face grew hot and my arms numbed and lost sensation. They became ballast, dead weight unable to mount a defense. What scared me most was not the prospect of life being choked out of me, but more the manner in which it was being accomplished. Unlike Talis' unintended violence, Harriet's viciousness was practiced and clean, efficient, like a curved road navigated a hundred times while blindfolded.

While in her grip, her eyes rolled back into her head, protecting themselves like those of a striking shark. Oddly, when she'd peaked ten minutes earlier, her eyes had also rolled back before she threw me off her body like a child's cloth plaything. Now, although her hands remained intent on ending me, their sinewy strength locked around my throat, there was something natural at play, a kind of balance that didn't seem out of place or unusual. I'd been looking for adventure, and to be in her hands in this way was part of the contract—an acceptable risk considering both the company I was keeping and my current state of undress. In that moment, light and darkness merged. By her grace alone, I lived another day.

Sometimes, when I closed my eyes tightly and let my mind wander, it was Delius lying beside me, on me, around me.

What was I looking for? A fair question. I was looking for nothing. I was looking for everything. I was looking for what was missing and that which was lost. Don't we all? Aren't we all drawn, in some manner, to that which is missing in us, for us, around us? If we're missing a drinking partner who carries our level of seriousness about the task, are we not drawn to the drinker and their dank and sticky haunts? If looking for conversation, do we not seek out a like-minded conversationalist, one who can carry a topic of our interest? And if it's attention we seek, even unknowingly, we are pulled toward the magnet of those who provide it to us, often to our detriment, at times to our destruction. Usually to our destruction.

Despite the constant progress of technology, the improvement in health and ever longer, more comfortable lives, we, as humans, are still ruled by base needs: food, water, air, a place to rest, socialization, procreation. And these needs, when interrupted, lead to irrational and unpredictable ends. When the algorithm runs its malignant calculations and spits results like an owl regurgitates the bones of its prey, there are always those whose needs are interrupted, whose dreams are left to rot in the field. And those dreams do not ride quietly into the sunset.

At first, it was the least I wanted, this affair with Harriet and not Delius (not that Delius would have me these days). But in slow but sure steps, Harriet became the one for me. She was the *something* that was missing. To say all I saw was Delius was no longer true. That's how it began, yes, but not how it ended.

"You think I'm her when you close your eyes," she said one day over dinner, one side of her face buried in a palm, her elbow on the flat of the table. "Even when your eyes are open, the way you look at me, it's like you're making up for lost time."

There was no point in hiding for there was nothing left to hide. "No," I replied. I couldn't keep the smile from my face. "I don't see her. Not anymore."

———

I recall one moment in particular where I caught sight of myself in the reflection of a bedroom mirror, working her pitted back with great and careful care. This time the room was well lighted and in the mirror I looked foolish, shoulders hunched while I skulked over her like an exposed night beast. How strange her scars and ridges were in the light, these very imperfections daring me to touch them. All the world had evolved, engineered to be ideal and perfect and just right: our eyes, our skin, our proportions, all were box-checked by our grinning, fastidious parents then chemically soaped and rinsed. Yet this imperfect being with her external flaws splayed before me—with her rising scent warming me—had become my infatuation.

Of those few who possessed flaws, the broken and scrambled eggs and the lemonade made from lemons, most would have hidden them, pushed away a hand or doused a light. Harriet did no such thing. She invited the exploration, pulled my hands to her back toward her secrets. Her secrets, and her back, were out front, unlike anyone I'd met.

One winter morning as a reddish sun rose and with our hair tousled from sleep (and more) and voices stale, Harriet, though unbothered, asked me why I wouldn't let go of her arm. Why did I always attempt to keep her in bed? In the near darkness, I spent a moment trying to decipher her question until I too noticed my hand clamped around her forearm, my grip sliding down to her wrist, stretching her arm to full length, tethering her as she attempted to flee. I hadn't realized I was doing it.

"How often do I do that?" I asked.

"Every morning," she said. "At least the mornings we're together."

"I guess I'm afraid if I let go, it will be the last time I touch you."

The words sprang from my lips without warning or conscious thought, though I didn't regret them, at least not fully. I'd never said anything like this to anyone. I'd never felt this way about anyone. I'd never wanted anyone to stay. You can't be abandoned if no one is ever invited to stay.

"You can touch me anytime you like," she assured me and kissed the tip of my nose.

She sat on the bed next to me, sensing I'd said more than I meant to, and placed her dry palm on my cheek. For a moment, she looked at me with that subtle kindness reserved for mothers, like I was still a boy. Then she whispered something strange, something I assume was meant as an endearment, but like much of what she said, it was foreign to me.

"You're mad as a hatter," she whispered and laughed. What an odd and unique and wonderful thing to say (whatever it meant!) Certainly, it wasn't what she said (the meaning was lost on me), but the way she said it—the curve of her lips, sincere and sweet, sending warm, gentle breath into my ear followed by a light kiss on my cheek. It was so delicate and magnificent; I couldn't be sure it happened.

Eventually, I realized why I pulled her back into bed each morning: I wanted her there, naked, her warmth beside me, close to me, if only to feel her a bit longer—to look at her just a little longer. To be happy.

"Do you think I aim to become a spinster?" she said once she'd broken free from the bed. "Someone who will run away from you?"

"A spinster?"

"Yes."

"I don't know what that is," I said.

"No?" she said and laughed again and, this time, pulled me up from the bed and into her arms. "Don't worry, I think you're the bee's knees!"

⸺

There was something else I haven't mentioned. Harriet's skin (though not the reptilian covering of her back)—it was softer than most, warmer and more delicate. When I ran a sharp fingernail down the length of her arm it left a thin pink trail, a distressed record of my tracing. After a few moments, the trail was no longer visible, fading slowly before disappearing entirely. It took some time for me to realize what was different, why her skin was softer, why it was warmer, why it had an attractive scent I can't find the words to describe: she didn't have a membrane. I'd never met anyone who wasn't protected by a thin layer of membrane. And, as I soon discovered, I'd also never met a woman who menstruated.

My first membrane was applied when I was five years old, at least according to the medical records. I have no specific memory of it. Although the membrane stretches significantly during our brief growth period, every ten years the membrane is reapplied and refitted, often with updated technology and performance improvements (at least according to the marketing brochure on the device). As the process evolved, the membrane was applied as a liquid. The thankfully warmed concoction is sprayed in a fine mist that slowly congeals. Only a few areas of the body are not treated: eyes, palms of the hands, lips, pads of the feet, ankles, genitalia, the back of the knees and pits of the elbows.

Before the membrane is applied, the subject is shaved clean, scalp and eyebrows, shiny skull and shorn arms, all smooth as an eggshell. The process is unnerving, though not particularly invasive. During the application of the membrane, the recipient is placed in a cylinder, strapped into a harness, goggled, and rotated around akin to being cooked on a spit at a county fair. A mist of membrane is interspersed with warm air to form an even coat and encourage drying. Once the application of the membrane is complete, the subject is chemically washed then spun and air-dried again.

Over time, as you outgrow the old membrane, you peel like a snake. Bits of silky, translucent evidence are shed here and there, under the sheets, in your socks, in the shower drain, sometimes in your food, more often jammed under your fingernails. Colloquially, it's called molting, and the anonymous doctors who scrape off the old membrane and then reapply the liquefied gold are known as "Molters." They call themselves God. It took a long time for me to understand why.

As you likely know, the primary (stated) function of the membrane is to prevent ultraviolet rays from aging and damaging skin. This very pragmatic function carries the added benefit of allowing the vain amongst us to preserve their youthful, vibrant appearance. The membrane also allows the body to regulate temperature by heating and cooling more efficiently. It's a miracle really, if you believe everything you hear.

There are rumors (there are always rumors when humans are involved) the membrane also delivers medication and the ten-year mark for membrane replacement is primarily to replenish the dosage. If we're to believe the conspiracy theorists, the membrane contains a slowly absorbed chemical that causes sterility, at least temporarily—in this case nearly permanent due to the duration of delivery. Is this scandalous rumor true? Is that how arrival is controlled among the masses? No one really knows. And no one really talks about it. And there's no one to ask.

Gossip is a most human endeavor, a ubiquitous form of pseudo-entertainment that has no cultural, educational or boundaries of class. And it can provide a useful societal function: it's a way to lower emotional temperature via distraction. Yet, we have lost our collective desire to gossip. Or, if not our desire, we have at least lost our willingness.

Nattering takes many forms: positive, negative, most benign—none of it matters now. The device is always listening. The device is always judging. We're afraid to allow the valve of stress to bleed and reduce the pressure—something the light words of chatter, yes gossip, often serves to do (despite the overwhelmingly negative connotations). Though, here I am, gossiping like I have nothing to lose. I have less to lose each day, but I'm not a rebel, and I'm too thin-skinned to support a specific cause. Wait, let me correct that statement. I've found Harriet with the mauve eyes and brown curls, so I have more to lose than I thought even yesterday.

It's curious this discussion of gossip seems so…gossipy.

It was also curious that Harriet, someone lacking a membrane, achieved the process of menstruation. It seems obvious now, doesn't it? But at that moment, there was no time to consider the connection and no reason to look for one. The conspiracy crowd is not big on coincidence. I was watching her sleep one morning, lying next to her with my elbow buried in the pillow, my cheek resting on the palm of my hand. I enjoyed watching her sleep (another odd thing to admit—I've become an impenitent voyeur!), her stomach rising and falling, her lips slightly parting with each exhale, the only sound was the moments being tallied one by one by the ticking antique clock on the dresser. I found I wasn't holding her arm. All was peaceful. I slid out of the warm bed to prepare breakfast, the soft pads of my feet cold against the floor, my careful steps meant to be unheard.

When I returned to wake her, there it was in all its glory! You can imagine my shock at the onset of this confusing and foreign process. I assumed she was in distress (what else would I believe!) and became sick to my stomach (I'm useless in an emergency.) Between retching contortions, I told the device we had "a situation." The device was confused. Though its scan of the apartment detected the presence (scent molecules) of blood and a slight increase in the temperature of the room, it asked for further clarification. As I paced the room in a suave, but unmistakable panic, I said Harriet was suffering a hemorrhage and was losing blood quickly and it was imperative someone hurried.

She awoke from a deep and restful sleep as my panic rose in both volume and intensity. She took note of my considerable weakness and, after chastising me, she attempted to reason with the device to call the whole thing off. There is no such thing as reasoning with the device. The light was now glowing a delicious red. What was done, was done.

Though the emergency team was initially as confused and concerned as I, Harriet communicated the relevant facts (she said we were being "wet rags") and the medical team, white gloves and oxygen masks, reluctantly exited the apartment without applying treatment. In the end, Harriet let out a wonderful laugh! She has such a wonderful laugh.

"I've seen blood to beat the band," she said and shook her head in grinning disbelief. "What's wrong with you? Are you a square? I've seen blood. That's not a lot of blood."

No, not a lot of blood to a seasoned soldier.

Talis
(The Dream)

reams often mirror the obvious—even for the oblivious.

The other morning, once Lark had dressed and gone, I dozed in and out of what—had it been a different day, or I a different person—one might consider a deep, satisfying sleep. Unremarkable, of course, but the reason I mention that particular morning is two-fold: first because it was rare that Lark spent the night and, second, due to the onset of a peculiar dream. There was about an hour of time between Lark rising from the bed and the device waking me. It was just enough time for my mind to both rest and race, to steal a few minutes of slumber while churning through the schedule of the day ahead. I'd achieved that cruel middle-ground of consciousness where often more questions are asked than answered.

The crux of the dream was this: I was wearing pink pajamas (not my own), standing alone in a field of long grass and yellow wildflowers when a masked man on a white horse rode in to save me—though from what event or state I required saving, I can't be certain. In the dream there was no obvious and present danger. I didn't feel or witness any particular distress and the world did not appear to be closing in upon me. All was normal to my eyes though real danger, the head of the snake, often provides little foreshadowing. True danger works in subtleties and innuendo, rides along in the undercurrent of everyday life, and percolates just below the water's surface. Sadly, we often miss the hints and fail to see the shards of glass hidden in the weeds before taking that regretted, barefooted step.

I also was not aware from where the man had rode. Was it from the East, West, North or South? Did it matter? There was neither an indication of his embarkation point, nor the reason for my apparent rescue being his sworn destination. I could see no observable reason for his grand arrival on horseback, nor any other back for that matter. Anyway, was he masked? Was he meant to hide from me or was it *me*? Was I not ready to know his identity? Lastly, what had summoned his regal services, and why?

The man was high up on the steed, confident, an exuberant white hat, gallons upon gallons, rested assuredly upon his head like it had been present since the birthing bed. Along with this hat, he was dressed almost entirely in white, and the sun was obediently staged behind him (so, it was East or West. But was it closer to sunrise or sunset?) and gave the angles and edges of his body a majestic, spectral glow. Even behind the mask he appeared handsome and self-assured with a chiseled chin and steely eyes.

His hands were costumed with pristine white gloves with

cut leather tassels that moved with ease…elegant without being extravagant. The only contrast was the black leather boots which were crisscrossed with off-white stitching. They rode to the top of his shins, ceasing just under the knees. The boots, too, were tidy and clean, shiny, like the dust they'd encountered on the ride was repelled by divine intervention. He looked like he'd been dressed by a movie costumer then been whisked away to a prop tent for the final shoeshine and glowing touches. Upon reflection, he looked rather silly.

As I mentioned, in this dream the man had come to rescue me, to raise me to the back of his steed, assure me of my safety and gallop away, perhaps even toward the sun. Was I in need of rescuing? I wondered—should I give in to this fantasy and let the course be taken?

The strange thing was (if this wasn't already strange enough), when I reached up to unmask my anonymous hero (as we all would), delicately removing the mask of white, he was Lark. What an odd and terrifying dream to be in want of being whisked away to somewhere else, to be saved and, presumably, brought to the safest place on earth only to find you're already there. Or did it mean there was no place to go—that no safe place existed? Or possibly it meant I had expected Lark to save me and he may yet. Or may not.

I've never been an interpreter of dreams and I wasn't ready for this. Perhaps I never would be. Looking back, there were questions I neglected to ask: was Lark meant to find me, was I his intended or did he get caught up in my rescue while passing through on his way to liberate another? Was this fate or a mission ill-fated?

Lark
(Absinthe)

Talis is gone. I let her go. She wanted to go. She just doesn't know yet. When I imagine releasing her, strangely, at the end of my evening while scraping my teeth with a new, fancy pumice brush, I can see her, clear and resolute like she's standing before me. She was always confident with blue eyes, straight spine, and thin lips. She walks with purpose, as usual, but there's something else. There's something she carries more and more often like a suitcase packed too heavily and it's causing an unnatural bend in her spine, a crick.

Contempt—that could be it. Contempt may be what I sense. She carries it in her heart, too. Her eyes are bulging and glassy now, angry, while her arms flail in great lofty arcs like she's knowingly swimming against an uncertain tide she will never fully tame. I'm safe, for now, in the cocoon of my imagination. In all this empty violence, she says nothing aloud though her mouth moves, forming vacant words and phrases. She's mouthing the words so only she herself can know her vile thoughts and her secrets. Vile. No, that's not a word I would use for Talis or about her—or about anything she does. She was never vile.

Long past denial, I, we, lug a gritty burlap sack filled high with our demons instead of a healthy, percolating uterus. This guilty sack swings freely, slung over a thin shoulder and shuttled home, stowed in a dark hallway closet until the sun rises again. The soiled burlap carries the weedy stink of failure—an odor of swamp and swill and decay. We were desperate in a world that does not reward desperation. We share this, being our disappointing "outie." I wonder if they'll throw a parade in our honor on a Saturday in November.

Whatever Talis' intentions, malicious or otherwise, I'm not the true reason for her callousness. Or at least that's what I believe. It's what I want to believe. Even in the whirl of my unsophisticated mind, it's Anna. Anna is the one who caught her unyielding glare, became the focus of her waking hours, her restless delusions. She is the reason for fighting the tide, attempting the doomed ocean crossing, even when there's no hope. It was always her. I just happened to be in the way. All becomes unclouded and dissembled to rudimentary pieces when we let go of what we once loved.

There is something, upon reflection, that Talis managed, something that made me itch my temple and pull my hair until the roots gave way. Yes, she used to tap her fingers along a desk, a table, any hard surface especially when she was deep in thought. Tap-tap-tap-tap, in reverse, from index finger to pinky, tap-tap. That was the worst of it. I had to clear my conscience and now it's settled. I mention this to highlight the imperfection of our existence. Yes, yes there are things that rattle us, get under our skin despite their insignificance—despite their small purpose. But it does not rise to the description of vile. You see, I'm still defending her.

Despite the contempt, Anna's not to blame. At least, not fully to blame. Though I've spent years being told otherwise, decisions were not of her making. If someone were to offer you that which was cherished by all, if you were presented your dream and all you need do was reach out and snatch it, would you not seize it with greedy hands, pull your arms tight and hug it with all your strength? We all would. But that's not what Anna did—she did not reach out a hand or elbow aside anyone who might interfere. What was offered to Anna was not known to be so rare, the relevance was hidden from her. She accepted, yes, but without knowing her acceptance would come at the expense of her sister. Would she have accepted her arrival even if she knew it meant Talis could not? She may have still, but it's all speculation. It's done. She's spent her life disfigured and for that alone, she may consider Talis to be vile.

For all our focus on perfection and genetics and splicing and stuffing what is desirable into our flesh, we're a feeble bunch. We're mentally weak precisely because we're not supposed to be. It's too great a burden to carry. The sack of demons is too unwieldy and the seams have begun to unravel and fray, to leak, the burlap worn thin with age. Human nature is not so easily unclouded and undone.

Yes, I'm into the absinthe again, the good bottle I keep under the basement stairs.

I've also accepted, or am working toward accepting, that despite decades of education and training, indoctrination and knowledge scraped up accidentally through the course of living, I've mastered little. I've mastered nothing. It could be a reckoning of a very distant past in which I've been informed by a yellow-lit report via the device that I possess, of all things, DNA passed down from Neanderthals. I've always been considered hard-headed and my knuckles have small, stiff hairs rooted to the surface, but I couldn't have imagined parts of my make-up, however negligible, is rooted in these brutes. I wouldn't doubt they'd say the same about me.

Worse still, I've also been told I carry sperm with scrawny, lopped off tails. These tiny fools have an oxygen-deprived sense of direction that causes them to swim in foolish, concentric circles, rendering them nearly incapable of reaching nature's goalpost. This stunted sense of direction manifests itself in other areas of my life, too. It takes me longer than most to find unfamiliar addresses or select a meal from a lunch menu. The Neanderthals are only partly to blame for my anguish.

(The Trench)

Trenches were dug forty feet long, ten feet deep and six feet wide using picks and shovels and metal buckets with the handles tied to frayed ropes. As soil was loosened, the buckets were filled, and those at the top of the trench pulled them up by the filthy ropes and dumped the soil into malignant hills of brown and black. These mounds of pregnant earth looked out of place, dotting the forest like a viral outbreak.

The trenches were usually dug near the bottom of a hill, and when an unscheduled rain arrived, they filled with mud and flotsam. After a rain, the trenches again needed to be picked and shoveled, raked and cleared. Part of the process. Part of the training. If no rain arrived, scheduled or not, explosives were set in holes bored into the side of the trench walls. Care was taken to assure the trenches were cleared of soldiers when the charges were detonated and the trench walls collapsed. Care, of course, was not a measurable attribute amongst the military brass. Either way, the trench needed to be cleared and the walls refashioned. Whether or not the dirt harbored bits of muscle and bone, possibly that of a friend as well as fellow soldier, was irrelevant.

The digger's fingers bled and dark soil was forced under jagged fingernails, leaving narrow black crescents at the tip of each finger. Though most bacteria were extinct, infections on the hands and feet, and in the eyes, were common. The skin of feet was rubbed raw by ill-fitting boots that filled with grime, mud, and rain. It reddened and swelled until they cracked and bleed. The unlucky ones at the bottom strained until their bodies broke and streams of sweat-soaked thin green uniforms were stained deep red with earth and blood. When a Captain indicated a solider was close to collapse, and only then, they were substituted with someone from the top, pushed up a ladder and attended by medics.

Over time, uniforms were whittled down to one—there was only military green—yet respect for rank—or what is interpreted as respect—lingered, especially among officers. It was critical for soldiers to know with whom they were speaking—the consequences were backbreaking. There were no shiny badges or colorful ribbons—no fancy jackets festooned with medals or stripes. There was only familiarity, and it was best to be up-to-date. It was imperative to be up-to-date.

The Captains were promoted from the soldiery, those with experienced backs fully scarred from service. There were rumors that Captains were considered and promoted only after an unknown number of confirmed kills, but the number, and the rumors, remained unsubstantiated. It was widely known an algorithm set by the device was largely responsible for the selection of officers.

Captain Walter wore military green with pride. Walter also wore a curved black sheath attached to his waist. Inside it held a knife with a blade curved near the tip, polished and sharpened to perfection. The end of the curved blade was forked like the tongue of an ancient liar. Attached to the outside of the sheath was a narrow, liquid filled cylinder about four inches long and the thickness of a thumb. The cylinder was divided into two sections with an opening on each end, both sealed with caps. Lastly, the black sheath hid a narrow, steel needle, pointed on one end and with a small eye on the other. It was widely considered a ceremonial dagger and not known to carry a purpose in combat.

On a Wednesday at dusk, Captain Walter looked up at the sky…something he'd done each day for the past three months. It was always a strange view, ten feet down and dark walls lurking on either side. The far end of the trench was barely visible in the fading light. The cloudless sky remained bright, streaked in red, orange, and blue. Looking upward from inside the earth gave the impression there were railings on the universe—borders—that it was a slice of something rather than an infinite space. There are always artificial reins in which we are placed, he thought, in which we exist.

The moon hung above the far end of the trench, a glowing dot on the trench's exclamation point. The sight of the moon spurred Walter to dream of lofty things. To him, the moon was freedom—whatever that meant—though he was proud to be a soldier, it was somewhere else, somewhere without trenches and walls and people and oxygen. People had died there in the not-so-distant past. Yes, there will always be death wherever you looked. Still, that's the place for me, he thought. If only I could reach it. Maybe, he considered, if you have to reach for it and still can't snatch it in your hand, then it is a dream.

At any given moment, there were seven soldiers in this trench, digging, and two at the top to hoist the buckets. There were no compelling work songs to help pass the time and no lively banter or hoots of comradery. There was only the silence of not being located by an enemy. Radio and magnetic communications were jammed, satellites blinded, infrared was dissipated, heat signatures were absorbed—there was only sound and there must be none.

At 2am, Captain Walter sat alone at the bottom of Trench Five-Sixty. His boots were covered in dark mud and in the darkness were indiscernible from the trench itself. His hands were numb from gripping a shovel handle, fingers curled and contorted, locked into shape, and a fleck of something (dirt?) was lodged in his right eye. He looked up toward the sky and blinked, hoping to dislodge the culprit, but the offending matter burrowed even deeper into his eye. He rubbed his eye with the sleeve of his shirt, but instead of providing relief, the mud-covered sleeve smeared a dark, gritty paste along his cheek. He decided on the spot to ignore it—what choice did he have? He was waiting for something to happen. Despite the time, now early morning, all remained quiet. Unusual. As far as he could remember, 1am was the latest for a Wednesday. Then again, this was part of the game, part of the training, part of the job. Expect it. It's coming. You just don't know when. Just don't be a fool and think it won't.

"You're not a fool are you, Walter?" the Sergeant-Major asked only last week, his eyes pressed into crescents like the filth under Walter's fingernails. He stood very straight with his arms pulled tightly across his chest but bent at the neck to focus on the soldier in the trench below.

"No, sir," Walter answered from the bottom of Five-Sixty, his voice full and confident. "I'm not a fool."

"Do you think I'm your friend, Walter?"

"Yes, sir."

"Then you're a fool!" scoffed the Sergeant-Major. "I like you, Walter, but I am not your friend. I will not invite you to my house for a holiday because we are not friends."

Walter knew if he'd responded differently, indicated he did not believe the Sergeant-Major was his friend, he would have received a similar reaction. And, knowing this, meant Walter was not a fool. It was the only thing Walter knew for sure.

"Tell me something, Walter," Sergeant-Major continued. "What's at the bottom of Trench Five-Thirty?"

"Our mission, Sergeant-Major," Walter answered.

"And what is our mission?"

"I'm sorry, Sergeant-Major, I cannot divulge the details of our mission."

"Do you know who I am?"

"Yes, sir, Sergeant-Major"

"Am I some sort of beatnik?"

"No, sir, Sergeant-Major."

"Am I a square?"

"No, sir," Walter answered. "You are the all-knowing, all-powerful, Sergeant-Major, Sergeant-Major"

"Then you will answer the fucking question!"

"I did, sir."

"Do you know why you carry the curved blade? Do you know who you are?"

"Yes, sir. I know who I am."

"Good man, Captain."

⎯

They heard it moving along the horizon—a benefit of living silently and working without making a sound is you always hear it coming. At 3am the nine soldiers of Trench Five-Sixty stood at the muddy bottom with approximately four feet of space between each of them. In the moments leading up to the attack, each prepared in their own way, their own custom or personal preference: a deep breath, the gritting of teeth, even a prayer to a deity bestowed with ethereal powers. Unlike the techniques to repel incoming fire, there was no longstanding military manual entry or instructional hologram on proper preparation for this type of attack—each was left to their own devices, their own acceptance.

"Curl up," ordered a voice from a drone hovering above the trench. "Protect yourselves!"

"Positions!" yelled the Captain. "Take your positions for incoming fire! Use your back to protect your front!"

Incendiary devices filled with reddish gel dropped from

the drone. Each device was met by the backs of nine soldiers on the bottom of the trench, each curled into a tight ball of weak flesh. Within seconds, the green military fabric was burned clean off, skin was scorched and darkened, pain was delivered and received. The wind carried the stench of charred flesh. There were no screams. There could be no sound. Even the insects were quiet, biding time.

The voice from the drone continued while the gel burned hot before settling into a soft, bubbling simmer. "If you're captured it will be worse. There's no mercy for Echoes. None. Learn from it!"

The night was cool and quiet save the buzz of drones moving into the distance, back toward the horizon. When they were out of range the insects renewed their eerie songs of the night and the soldiers slowly uncurled.

—

On that same Wednesday, twenty miles to the south, a soldier sat in the mud at the bottom of trench Four-Twenty. She'd spent the last half-hour cleaning the wounds on another soldier's back, stitching the lacerations caused by a surprise artillery volley that followed an incendiary attack. Once the bleeding was controlled and stitches applied, she smeared burn cream and antibiotic—then applied liquid skin to prevent infection.

"Clean," Harriet said as she blew air onto the liquid skin to help it congeal, to help it seal the skin.

"Thank you," the other solider said with a smile before

fetching a fresh shirt from a green, waterproof bag and melting away into the far end of the trench.

"You need to remember to duck," Harriet joked before he was out of sight.

"Thanks for the tip," he said and smiled over his shoulder.

Though she'd also received wounds that night, Harriet didn't feel pain. There was no pain emanating from the unhealed bones of her neck vertebra, or the sores of her infected feet, or anywhere that she could recall. There hadn't been for a long time. When did this begin? When did the pain cease to be painful? She couldn't be sure. One morning she awoke to the strange sensation of nothingness. Everything, her body, all of her person felt…fine. She searched her body for the usual aches using the thin skin of her palms, patting her body with her hands and tracing with her eyes: knees, hips, the small, swollen joints of each finger. Nothing. Even the pain from the long festering wounds of her back had faded into memory.

To evolve into a good soldier, she considered, requires physical pain, the threat of it, be set aside, ignored, banished to…somewhere else. I am a good soldier, she thought. I will strive to be better.

There was still pain, however, though it was no longer the physical sort. What she desired most, above all, was not to rise in the military ranks or become a celebrated hero, but simply to serve and die with a soldier's honor. Though she understood their necessity, she didn't care for drills and training and monotony. She wanted to be in the middle of the action. Despite the inherent dangers, she wanted to make things happen, to make a difference to whatever ends. The thought of anything less and a concern she may fall short were her constant companions.

She understood her purpose. She'd also heard of citizens who spent their entire lives waiting to fulfill their purpose—to reproduce. She pitied them, their soft bodies and weak minds, willing slaves to an algorithm and dinner with a stranger seated across the table, someone they used to know but no longer loved. That's not for me, she concluded long ago.

Several requests to transfer into the intelligence service were met with a disappointing yellow-light of "wait." Despite her insistence and willingness, including her experience, the change she was eventually granted was not what she'd expected. Instead of a transfer, she was granted, according to the details of the report, a release from service. In essence, she was granted her freedom. She'd requested a position in which she could immerse herself in her craft and was rewarded, in her eyes, with exile. It was disappointing that her life, as well as her death, would not be of her own choosing.

In the weeks leading up to her scheduled release and integration into society, she carried the heavy burden of a weighty lack of purpose. Her usual run, jack-rabbiting from here to there and her signature frenetic pace, was replaced by a slouched, foot-dragging gait. She had little desire to enter society, to lounge in a comfy chair and watch the sunset each evening, warm absinthe in one relaxed hand, not a care in the world in the other. She loathed the thought of spending her remaining days in a pampered comfort and safety. She saw little value in being a citizen…a commoner. Now, she too would be under the device's invisible thumb as a slave to its electricity, its circuitry, and whims.

There was something else, another secret that embarrassed her…a desire, she feared, that made her no better than the others. No freer. Before her soldier's death, before her honor was enshrined, she wanted to spend a few moments hopeless in rapture. She wanted to feel the sweetly acidic sting of Cupid's arrow piercing her flesh…love. Just once, for a short time before her name was called, she wanted to spend every waking hour with someone, to be lying next to him when the final lights were dimmed and she ceased to feel anything at all. Yes, she thought, an old-fashioned, hopeless romantic like she'd read about, like the ancient movies before color. Only then would she allow the physical pain to return and allow him to soothe it. A hypocrite, perhaps, but it's what she wanted before her life was snuffed out by a bullet or pulverized by an artillery shell. Or before her throat folded under an assassin's blade. Or worse.

The dread of being abandoned to society, leaving the service she'd known all her life, kept her awake at night. When sleep was elusive, she stared up at the flat, smooth ceilings of the military dormitories, toward the thousands of stars under an open field, or within the slice of sky cut into a trench. Her appetite faded and she could barely stomach her daily rations. Each morning her stomach was turned inside out as she considered her upcoming transfer…her "reward." Even the skin of her back, reptilian and disfigured, began to ache again and split like a molting snake, oozing wet pustules that clung to the fabric of her uniform. This was not how she envisioned her end. And it made her angry.

However, during the last few weeks of her scheduled service, she was assigned to Trench Five-Thirty under the command of Captain Walter. At the bottom of trench Five-Thirty, ankle deep in reeking mud and silence, with no one to bear witness and no physical pain, everything changed.

—

It should be noted: Soldiers, Echoes, by law, were forbidden to procreate. They were physically capable, more so than most in open society—their sperm could swim and dive and frolic, and their eggs were viable, healthy, and enduring. They were physically fit and, as with members of society, were generally immune to myriad disease. Despite controls, it was a matter of when, not if, there would be reproduction of Echoes. There were rumors—since everyone knew someone that knew someone—that those caught participating in forbidden activities, whether successfully or not, were transferred to the infantry, no questions asked. On the front lines the rate of return, the chances of survival were zero. Ironically, the ones sent to die, were branded "bad eggs" by the device. It was cold and calculated and necessary, like the Echoes themselves.

—

These opinions were expressed in a note written by Captain Walter to Harriet at the bottom of Trench Five-Thirty during an evening of scheduled rain. The runoff filled the wounded earth with mud and washed in decaying leaves and bits of broken branches:

The relative peace of society carries costs not revealed on the daily updates from the green-lit device. Society is blind to it, going about their dreary lives, their day-to-day, myopic and therefore ignorant. In some ways, they're not at fault, as they're selected as we're selected. Peace demands force and force demands a standing army and the burden falls upon the unfortunate souls splayed from the whole, the ill-fated side of the divided egg, a fifty-fifty cleave of fate. Yet, in many ways, we're the lucky ones, dropped into a life of violent simplicity while the other half develops psychological toxicity, enduring concerns about meals and careers and children and surgery to replace this or that or to unclog this of that. To have a life free of the burden of family, free of disappointments from academic ineptitude or artistic failure, to not require the weight of relationships is a gift we must embrace. We have the power to take life while they strive to create it. We are the narrow blade of the sword, honed sharp by skilled hand, while they are the blunt, fleshy hand that struggles to wield it. We have an end, an expiration date, a use-by label carved into the small of our backs. It's what we look forward to, what we aspire to meet. In many ways, it's our gift. We are not meant to overcome our station; we are meant to be our station. In the meantime, while we endure, we must remain useful.

The movements and missions of the military remain secret. Even the device is not amongst us as there is always the opportunity for unexpected ears and careless mouths. While the military leadership works hand in hand with those who control the device, we are free of its daily reach. We are not bound by its whims of colored lights.

Talis
(Frisky)

"Would you really want to live past one-hundred-forty?"

That was my father's question one evening over dinner. He was leaning toward me for effect, his hands looping in air independent of his body, his chair leaning forward on two brittle legs. "At that point, you're seeing a mechanic, not a doctor. Someone who switches out the original part for a shiny new one. Zip-Zip. Is that what we want…to be a little less ourselves each passing day?"

Over the past century, an unprecedented number of diseases were mitigated by science. The known cancers, for example, were largely a scourge of our ancestors, as were most, but not all, viruses. Bacteria, at least in society, was mostly controlled. Typical modern deaths were from reasons of organ failure: old, unoiled organs worn down from use rather than a succumbing to specific disease. Or, seemingly as often, it was a person's choice to leave, a form, signed and initialed here and here and verified by eye-scan, indicating they wished to depart on their own terms.

When threatened however, nature has a way of conjuring something new in its simmering black cauldron, something previously hidden and often fatal. Just like our dreams of conquering the moon, our dream of conquering disease remains a foolish, dangerous endeavor. For once we believe we've resolved something previously unresolvable—a mend for this or a procedure for that—nature saves its most sinister ailments for that which is least accessible and still largely misunderstood: the brain. The score will never be even as there is always something worse waiting in the shadow—a new trick—a new deception. The game is unbalanced and not in our favor. And, if by chance, we do pull even and manage to keep pace, nature will change the rules of the game.

I watched my father's hands deteriorate over many years. Where once they were strong hands, honest and smooth, they became the twisted hands of a troll, fingers curled inward (some outward) unable to straighten. Large, festering bumps and swells of inflammation took residence in every knuckle and every tendon was stretched and torn. When he could no longer manage the pain, a laser cut slices of rot out of his knuckles and replaced it with lab-grown resin and pixie dust. All this in one afternoon. He was guilt ridden for his relief and felt like he he'd stolen another man's hands, lopped them off at the wrist while the man slept off a night of too much absinthe only to awaken in pain and loss and without hands to wipe the sleep from his eyes. No problem. The lab will grow more. Always more.

Though I hadn't considered it until recently, in time, his internal discomfort became my comfort. Such an unusual thing to savor.

"You'd want Anna to live to two-hundred," I said to him. I was feeling frisky and my nose itched which indicated I was ready for a fight.

"Please don't be angry with Anna," he pleaded. "She's your only sister. The algorithm takes many things into account. I would assume being the first born is one of them."

"You had two children. You arrived twice. Seems peculiar, doesn't it?" I'd mastered the subtlety by now—the nuances of the victim. It was all I had left in my control. Yes, I was very frisky.

"Those were different times, Talis," he said, his lips pulled thin across his face, pulling away their color until they were pale white. "Everything has changed."

Yes, and nothing has changed.

I can no longer sleep. I can't recall my favorite color. I don't know if my underwear is clean.

I want my bed.

Fear the device. Love the device.

Love to fear the device.

⌒

What is normal? Has our definition evolved over millennia like the elongating beak of a Darwin inspired fowl? People in ancient books seem so different from us—windy and far away, like the words they desperately want to speak need to be cleaved from other dusty books more ancient than themselves. They never seem happy or content—orphans who only dream of becoming rich and revered or the offspring of well-to-do parents who long to linger in the world of the common folk—if only to obtain the practical, even pious, touch of the commoners. Their time is either spent attempting to secure (often with foolhardy results) what we take for granted: homes, careers, food, safety, leisure and entertainment, or, in the case of those who have their needs already met by their forebearers, morality and emotional continuity. It's exhausting. And far-fetched.

The ancient's finite time flitters away with what can best be described as worry and insecurity. Conflict. Yet, they possess, often in wild gradations and sometimes reluctantly, what we—what I—yearn to have: control. Control, to a large degree, over their path, their future, their forward, whichever direction they chose. There lies the great divide. We, us, society, have made a bargain, a covenant, trading control away for perceived comfort and security. We are sacrificial pawns on a preordained chessboard. How strange. How foolish the ancients all seem to me. They fret about homes and cars and what their neighbors possess, their petty grievances debated in chilly stone buildings by hired experts of law festooned in wigs and robes, the twentieth century's court jesters. The scrolls of law became what stone walls and wooden fences were to their predecessors, even if they were blissfully unaware of it at the time.

I sound like my father delivering an impromptu lecture across the table over dinner, banging his meaty, reddened fist to emphasize a point, before realizing he's frightened his audience into a silent submission. Of course, I never went silently—at least not in my head.

Speaking of dinner, there's no reason for it. The act of eating, the physical act of eating is obsolete. It should have been lost to time like yellowfin tuna and hummingbirds and weak chins and attached earlobes. If not for the concepts of family and socialization, dinner would have gone the way of such outmoded constructs as political parties and struggling artists. It would have run its course and been forgotten, lost to Darwinism and good manners. However, I'm told there is the practical need to prevent atrophy in the body, to work things, to keep them moving for fear of losing them. If we were not to use the muscles of our mouth, our esophagus, our stomach and intestines and all the rest, they would shrivel to raisins and lose what limited function remains. This would be most unpleasant in such an emergency where basic needs were not being met, though it's been decades since the infrastructure failed and we were left to fend for ourselves.

There is a movement promoted by those called Revisitists—I'm not sure if that's what they call themselves or what everyone else calls them—to rediscover ourselves, our past selves, our ancestral selves, i.e. to revisit our humanity. We're living creatures with certain hardwired needs and many Revisitists (not of the political variety) believe in reconnecting with our past behaviors as these connections are considered soothing to the psyche. The Revisitists, the dedicated ones at least, are said to be headquartered in the wild mountains where they revisit and reconnect and regurgitate what is old as new. Rumor has it they live off the land, with the land, which means, I assume, in the mud. On occasion, their influence, however benign, infiltrates society and sends us scurrying to reconcile our lifestyles. They used to call these things "fads."

Some of these attempts to reconnect to our primitive selves, our "revisits," were considered either outlandish or just plain silly. Take for example, the brief experiment in which bottles of milk (from cows! In glass bottles!) were delivered to our homes each day. And this, without having to make a request via the device. This delivery of milk was left in an insulated metal box with a hinged lid! On the porch or near the front door! Was this the zenith of frivolity or a legitimate attempt to recreate the comfort of a home from numerous decades and centuries of the past? I may as well have rubbed my face raw with coal dust or stood near an antique microwave oven to receive a suitable dose of radiation. Would a dose of radiation from those primitive devices have brought me closer to our ancestors, had a "walk in their shoes" as the saying goes? And did I really want to be closer to those corpulent imposters, to their alleged happiness, stomachs stuffed swollen with cakes and sauces, the skin of their feet dry and peeling. And the odors, these commuters of work, I can hardly imagine them, garlic and perspiration teaming up to offend after a day, shoulder to shoulder, on a sweltering passenger train. I think not.

I guess the question is why? What was the goal? Was it to bring back some of the old things, some of the things that, for their reasons or some logic, made us nicer to each other and more social? Was this the so-called "Secret Sauce?" Was this the key to unlocking our misplaced humanity? And what did the delivery of cow's milk mean to accomplish? The "milkman" they once called him or her. What an odd remembrance of the past to resurrect. He made his way each morning, this surefooted man, a hat of white listing atop his head and a dull blue smock with a name-patch, "Frank" in curly script, sewn in place. The truck, determined and refrigerated, roared to a stop in front of each home and delivered (I still can't believe it) that which came from the depths of actual cows! Did this small gesture, a chilled bottle of milk (perhaps teeming with ancient bacteria) awaiting us each morning, return a sense of civility to our lives? Was it an olive branch to the lives of our friends and neighbors? Was it meant to restore our humanity? I can't say, for I can't recall what that was like having never known it myself. It was not the last nor the first attempt to reclaim our humanity through bizarre revisits, but it's one that stuck with me. It was a short-lived experiment.

There was something else I noticed about our ancestors, especially from books and visual entertainment—they were obsessed with violence and murder. I don't mean to imply they were inherently violent or murderous, but rather their entertainment tended to feature events that glorified such behavior. Why? Surely, we've learned human nature works in a cycle, but this focus lingered for far longer than one would expect. While the world slowly became a less danger-ous place, our longing to be surrounded by interpretations of it remained. It was almost like they loved the something they feared the most, like being terrified of ghosts and purposely spending the night in the attic of a haunted inn. Or being afraid of the device. Perhaps a cool glass of recently delivered, bacteria-laced cow's milk took the edge off.

Talis
(A New Job)

After much consideration, agonizing thought that wrestled away already elusive sleep and reddened my eyes, I accepted Anna's offer to join the Office of Acclimation. It wasn't really an offer, at least in my mind. It was more of a favor, and Anna was quite aware of it. The truth is, I needed something to occupy my mind and to consume the excess oxygen, tripping up any running thoughts and slow the inching of a creeping madness. Each passing new year was more difficult, the yellow light deeper, denser, and I grew less accepting, and as I'm sure you long ago concluded, angrier. In that moment of decision awake at 3am, nerves of my arms deadened and useless, I wore anger like a second skin and it was gradually becoming more comfortable.

In the past, when a distraction was needed, I dove head-long into projects at the office. Typically, these tasks were the ones no one else wanted to tackle, that were deemed too labor intensive to induce a flurry of volunteers or worse, be assigned to friendly faces by a timid Mid-Lev. This method had served me reasonably well, occupying my days and often my nights. It was far easier to work through the night than attempt a sleep that refused to heel. In this, I became something of an office star, at least in my eyes. At home though I continued my career as the pariah, and Lark's assessment of our corresponding home life was much, much dimmer. I justified it under the moniker of sacrifice. It was also a distraction to be sure. As expected, this new position in the service of Anna, required more sacrifice, but of a much different kind.

On my first day, Anna greeted me at the security desk to supervise my body scan. Her attendance was an unnecessary gesture, but like delivery of milk onto one's porch, it was part of some new, personal touch theory the Office of Acclimation was trying on for size. The device had already transmitted my particulars, so it was a reasonably quick and painless process (i.e. no yellow or red lights). Afterward, as Anna and I walked to the elevator, she informed me with her uncanny airs of societal superiority that she wouldn't be my direct superior in the Office of Acclimation. It wasn't her decision, but she was in full agreement. How nice. The pitch of her voice dipped and rose so I couldn't tell if she was disappointed or relieved, but I know which one I preferred.

"That wouldn't be appropriate, now would it?" she said in a half-sneer, half-laugh, upper lip curled up toward her nose, the ubiquitous pink scar nearly lost in the pale folds of her forehead. Was she trying to be reasonable or just attempting to appear reasonable like a skilled politician who'd lost the recent cabinet vote on her newest scheme, but was being careful to preserve some goodwill for the future? I found my hands were curled into tight, clammy fists whenever Anna spoke or was within striking distance. The muscles of my neck and shoulders grew tense, causing the back of my head to ache. As a calming exercise, I reminded myself of family and decorum and the wonders of sisterhood. It helped little, if at all. One favor, however robust and well-meaning, does not untether a lifelong curse from a sturdy hitching post.

The first several days were spent in the obscurity of Training Pod 7, shut off from the outside world, immersed in the nauseating rigors of manuals and procedures, rules and regulations. It was indoctrination at its unsettling finest, depredation and starvation—the manifesto of modern business and the drumbeat of the Mid-Lev. It was torture akin to having a handful of hornets shoved down my blouse, though I couldn't decipher whether Anna was the hand or the hornets.

I'm not sure if Pods 1 through 6 were already assigned or if I was the only new trainee being tortured. Or maybe Training Pod 7 was the only one dedicated to the Office of Acclimation with whatever deviance was in store for me. Or maybe there were no other training pods. Maybe Pod 7 was all they'd built despite grand plans for 1 through 6 and 8 through 10. Those were the questions I considered instead of focusing on whatever nonsense was being transmitted to me and at me: flashing lights, numbers, projections, axioms, slogans, rules, measures. By the end of each day, all I absorbed were blurred images (and burned retinas), a whirlpool of facts and figures whittled for my petty consumption. At best, I was a poor student. At worst, I would evolve into a poor employee. It felt good to have goals.

Each time I fell asleep in Pod 7 (which was more often than I'd care to admit), the chair vibrated, the earpiece buzzed, and the lights flickered in bright, gamey colors. It was more like a reward given for providing a correct answer on the set of an old-time game show than a slap on the knuckles meted out by peeved training software. It was grammar school and poison ivy all over again. Every hour, on the hour, I swore I'd learned my lesson. "It won't happen again. I swear." Consistency, at least, was on my side.

By the end of the first week, I'd grown numb to it all. My mind floated in a dozen different places, hovering in a hundred moments of the past and a thousand moments of the future, as impossible as it all seemed. Despite the white walls and rounded texture of the pod's furniture, all feverishly designed to minimize distraction, I remained thoroughly and I feared permanently distracted. I rose from my bed each morning wanting to learn, to dive in, to keep my mind active with work, but the cement wouldn't set, the replacement organ wouldn't take, the patient was critical. I wondered, aloud and often and to myself, if I'd made a mistake in accepting this position. After all, did I really want to see Anna's smug little face every morning and afternoon?

Each afternoon I was summoned to Anna's office to review the skills I was expected to learn rote. Each afternoon, I recalled very little of the previous several hours. The hours spent in Pod 7 were no more than a misty morning or a swirl of wet paint. Consistency. I wanted my bed and my pillow and my blanket. I wanted to be home. Alone. Making a good impression at the office was off to a turbulent start, yet I'd barely taxied to the runway. My office star faded in the night sky, in Anna's sky.

Anna prowled a strange little office, stark white and almost oval in shape. There was one small, round window that comported itself like a decommissioned ship's dingy porthole. The porthole overlooked numerous other portholes that peered out of other strange little offices. Taken in totality, the windows looked like bubbles floating upward through a corn silo. There was grey nothingness outside the porthole (and the other portholes) other than a sliver of ancient light mandated by some obscure mandate long ago negotiated by the aforementioned wigged and robed lawyers. If the porthole could be opened (it could not), I could have touched the outside wall of the next building with outstretched fingers. Sadly, I was sure Anna's office provided far superior natural light than whatever windowless and dusty corner I'd be assigned in due time.

We sat across from each other, she in her gracious executive chair perched behind an unnecessarily large, but oddly empty desk, oval like the room. With a silent flick of her wrist, I was directed to a worn fabric chair, brown with cold metal arm rests like a chair reserved for ill-behaved children and employees who'd hit a bump while in the midst of their probationary period. There was a lecture in the air, and the stench was unmistakable. She was her father's daughter.

"You need to try and pay attention," she said in an exasperated manner too much like our mother, her arms crossed tightly on her chest, her posture stiff, upright before a flat palm hit the top of the desk for effect. She was exercising her ample family gifts: the worst of both parents.

"I will," I said. I didn't mean it. Anna knew I didn't mean it.

"As your sponsor, I need to make sure you're up to it."

"Of course. I understand."

"Don't make a fool of me, Talis."

"No. Never. We're sisters." I shrugged. I'm not sure why I tortured her. Hadn't I done enough?

Anna tried to relax in my presence, crossing her legs with undue heaviness and dissatisfaction, then uncrossing them, crossing her arms again (like dear mother), then dropping them to her lap when she became conscious of the too-close-to-home mannerisms. She conjured breathing exercises from her dossier of corporate tricks, deep and determined breaths, her chest ferociously expanding like a lizard's dewlap before whistling in withered deflation. It did little to mitigate her anxiety. It may have increased it.

While looking toward the porthole that overlooked nothing, she itched her scar with a long, dry finger, poking a sharpened nail deep into the crevasse. She was hiding something and not particularly well. It was our father's old trick.

"There's something else," she said and faked a satisfied smile, a winner's smile.

"I'm sure there is," I said and returned the smile, a second-place smile.

"I want you to meet someone. His name is Walter. I think you'll like him."

(The Parade)

For as long as anyone could remember, a parade was held on the third Saturday in November. It was a grand affair proceeding down every Main Street, over every notable bridge named after a notable person and into every town square. It was roundly considered the highpoint of the year's civic life—a not-to-be-missed event and the place to be seen. Though officially called The Arrival Parade, it was colloquially known as the *Parade of the Uterus.*

Rain was rescheduled to the week after the event and the temperature was carefully moderated for everyone's comfort. The streets were cleared of everything from transports to dining tables and scrubbed with silicon until they glowed. Buildings and sidewalks were double molted clean to show their quality. Even the trees were dusted and pruned. Ribbons of every size and hue were hung in windows along the parade route, and banners were strung from building to building at every height from the 10th floor to the 500th and even higher. The sheer volume and crisscrossing of banners between buildings and across streets gave the impression a very large spider had spun a very large web. It was a time of earnest celebration and everyone, every parent and child, every grandparent and aunt and uncle, every friend of a friend, was encouraged to attend.

A voluptuous green light emitting from the device—the second green of the year for those lucky couples—served as the formal invitation for marchers. For the invited, the lucky and the newly arrived, the invitation, however lighthearted, was not optional. While costumed as an invitation (who wouldn't welcome a green light?), this second green was an official summons to march and to demonstrate to the world the culmination of your arrival—the growing fetus, be it an "innie" or an "outie." It was also meant to demonstrate to the world arrival was not only possible, but thriving, that each and every year citizens arrived. People just like you(!) had this great gift bestowed upon them.

Rest assured, your time will come! Yes, you!

Maybe even next year!

Lost in the celebration and confetti and buried in the pomp and circumstance of the day, was the fact each uterus emitted two distinct heartbeats. Twins, after all, were not a reason to celebrate. The gestating dowry was best unmentioned.

Most citizens were thrilled by the opportunity to march. They were having a good year (indeed!) —and it was important to look your best. Soon, tailors were commissioned to fashion new outfits, cobblers were busy creating shoe lasts—busy feet needed new shoes. All of the fashion world and the requisite tabloids were abuzz in the months preceding the annual parade. It was the place to be seen and the place for both designers and social climbers to show their quality.

One woman (an innie) during her year, wore an out-fit designed by none other than Vladimir Tsokevsky! It was a silk evening gown, jet black and infused with diamond dust and Andromeda starlight…a one-shoulder masterpiece with sparkling shoes to match! Her ruby-red pupils and ivory skin, when cast against the black and starlight, proved irresistible to the camera's eye. She waved and thanked the gawking spectators, smiled and nodded her head, posed for photographs and holograms alongside her husband, dapper in his all-black tuxedo. Her parents, giddy beyond words, picked up the sizable expense of the gown and shoes without regret. The tabloids ate it up. Among the myriad headlines were "Lady Starlight" and "Rubies Sent from Heaven." She was the woman of the hour, if only for an hour. Tomorrow, she'd be forgotten.

The outies too, were dressed in elegance formally reserved for weddings and fundraisers for the cultural elite in shimmering gowns and black-tie tuxedos. They of course, had the added challenge of making their mark by high-lighting their now percolating uterus, which was no easy task. Some creative types hired artists who used specially formulated uterus paint to create living (often moving) uterus murals, colorful and intricate, constantly in flux and as varied as life itself. One particularly brave and memorable attendee had her surgically extended uterus fashioned into a gelatinous hat (by design mogul Imogen Bonadova no less!) and balanced it, carefully, on her head over the entire course of the parade route.

Citizens lined the street a hundred deep and over-filled the windows and balconies a hundred stories high along the route. All were cheering in full throat to welcome the present and future, hoping to catch a glimpse of the expectant parents in full stride as this year's ripened crop. To say it was the social event of the season is to sell it short and minimize the impact, even if everyone in attendance knew it was all a device-centric spectacle. They knew deep down it was a farce conjured up by those in the shadows, the specters flipping the switches and turning the knobs.

There were even a few older couples in the parade, some in their eighth or ninth decade, who had long given up but were cleverly selected to provide a ray of hope for those still crippled by the tepid yellow beacon of "wait." They didn't mind. It was important to project this thin ray of sunshine and sliver of hope to the damaged psyche of those in society who, thus far, were unable to fulfill their most ardent wishes.

For those unable to attend, the device (never missing a chance to broadcast a spectacle) carried the event live, beaming it to every household. Sporting events were cancelled. Theater and arts came to a grinding halt. Entertainment ceased. Everyone gathered around the nearest device to watch.

Everyone, of course, saw what they wanted to see: The future saw their upcoming arrival festooned in elegant designer outfits, swooning fans a million strong, mouths agape, a society ready to welcome them. The present saw their time, their moment, a thrilling culmination of patience and perceived sacrifice. The past saw their children carrying their future grandchildren, life renewed, their legacy carried forth in the form of the next generation. The unarrived, those old enough to understand and suffer, saw it as pure spectacle, with unfairness and hopelessness and absurdity. Another year had passed them by.

Anna and her younger sister, Talis, were in attendance in their early years, often one perched upon their father's shoulders while the other squeezed through the hip-to-hip crowd to find a favorable viewing spot on the sidewalk. One particular year, the girls wore matching red velvet dresses and, as an added treat, had their hair styled at their mother's salon. If it was a day to be seen, they wanted to be part of the scene.

Years later, Anna would recall the look on Talis' face as she watched the newly ordained celebrities walk in a practiced, elegant gait, each outfit determined to outshine the others. There was awe and excitement and pomp and pageantry. Three decades later, Anna herself would receive an invite to the parade. Sadly, Talis would not.

Not unexpectedly, the sisters' relationship began to rupture and contort. In the years after Anna marched, Talis kept an admirable, decadent distance from her sister, like she was a painting that begged to be fawned over but would stain and deteriorate if touched by acidic fingers or the warm breath of decaying teeth.

A boy named Lark was at the parade once too. He was a shy, emotionally distant child with dry, pink lips and curly brown hair. He hid under his mother's tartan shawl for most of the parade, closing his eyes tightly in hopes it would all be over. When he finally opened his eyes and emerged from her shadow, he gave the event a cursory once-over and moved on. He was too disinterested for his parents to return the following year.

Talis
(Meeting Walter)

Such an old-fashioned name: Walter. And such an odd person. He speaks as if he were born decades or maybe centuries ago with these little amalgams of words that make no sense to anyone but him. I had to ask him what he meant by some of his peculiar expressions, though it seemed at times he didn't know himself. To many of my requests for clarification, he just laughed like he'd invented them on the spot for my benefit and amusement.

Walter has a wonderful laugh.

The thing is, for as many times as I tortured Anna, tugged at the loose strings of her person until they were sore and began to unravel, she returned the favor tenfold. But in this case, she was right, I did like Walter—his dimples and curly brown hair, his rust-colored eyes (when the light caught them just so), the way his lip twitched when he drank something hot, the way he looked at me when he spoke like I was the only person in the world. He reminded me of Lark before...

Well of course he did—he was Lark.

Only he was Walter.

And of Lark, the actual Lark, I didn't know where he was. I'd lost track of his comings and goings. Certainly, it was all spoiled milk (I got that one from Walter) and it was likely the marriage was over. Neither of us had bothered to ask, so I guess that's its own manner of confirmation. Now I was assisting his Echo at Anna's request. She certainly had a flair for the dramatic.

Anna explained Echoes were twins, cut, chemically spliced (whatever) from one egg. This dividing, however it was accomplished, was payment, a dowry, for one's arrival and given willingly by the desperate and the young, people like my parents and Anna. And me. Only not me. Not yet. Maybe never.

What an elegant system of sacrifice, splitting an egg into two: one for the betterment of society, one for its protection. If that's not the official slogan at whatever fucking office concocts official slogans, they should adopt it immediately. I resolved to dictate it to the device that very evening, but I doubt I remembered. I don't remember if I remembered. As it turns out, I didn't really care that much.

Love the device. Fear the device.

Before meeting Walter, I'd assumed an Echo would be different—more artificial and stiff—more like a coffee maker than the coffee, born to take commands, and save a few beeps and dings, sit quietly on a kitchen counter until needed. Of that most unique of human qualities, our eyes, I expected to be staring into the glassy yellow eyes of an owl—a killer's hollow eyes, lacking a soul, shallow and feck-less. But Walter was flesh and blood and more. His eyes were more human and brighter than my own. He was, well…he was just lovely.

Why was it that Anna assigned me to Walter and him to me?

"Walter was originally assigned to me," she explained in well-rehearsed, passive aggressive Anna-ese. "But passing him along to you seemed more…interesting."

Another torture conjured from her simmering cauldron, eye of newt and blood of toad. Bitch.

There were other Echoes under my guidance—five in total including Walter. But the other four held no station with me. They were ordinary and parochial and barely worth mentioning. I conducted myself in that mothy civil servant manner, tepid and even-keeled, fluttering about with no particular destination in mind to keep them on their toes. I did my job. I found them housing, employment, taught them life skills, things like interacting with the device and making coffee and cutting their toenails often. I listened to their confusion and their foolish sayings that made little sense, smiling along, nodding like a proud aunt despite their embarrassing antics. They were all at least a little strange. Mostly, I kept them on the straight and narrow path. Except for one. Him. Walter. I devised other plans for him.

Despite my repeated mantra, the reminders to myself

that it was a just a job (not to mention the lectures of Pod 7), I found myself not only knee deep, but neck deep. But this wasn't about them or him. It was about to become about me.

Walter made the worst coffee. At first, his coffee was acceptable, tasty even, but over time, it regressed, becoming almost undrinkable. A strange observation, I agree. And, if this were his biggest flaw, he'd be far ahead of his twin. Another strange observation, I agree. The thing is, Walter made me forget about Lark. And remember him. All at the same time. Mostly, I found myself not thinking about Lark at all…even on the infrequent nights Lark returned home for reasons I haven't asked about, sleeping beside me. No, not beside me. That implies a willingness and consciousness about it, like twenty years ago. No, he sleeps near me. Even on the nights he sleeps near me, he doesn't enter my thoughts.

On those nights, I cower to one side of the bed, pull the warmed covers toward me, and wrap myself in a tight, impervious cocoon. But it wasn't out of fear of what may happen or what shenanigans may unfold. There's a foggy guilt I can't put my finger on…a vague feeling that Walter wouldn't approve of our proximity should I allow a damp foot to touch his or a rogue arm to drape heavily across his chest. Why would I be concerned about such frivolous things at my age? He's my husband, after all. And why would I concern myself with something trivial like Walter's approval?

Anyway, I'd taught Walter the mechanics of the coffee machine, not really much more than fingering a few buttons and wobbling a few levers. He seemed to understand the instructions and even asked the device for the instruction manual so he could study it in the evening, which was a habit born of the military, I'm sure. Months later, his skills had not improved. I should probably laugh, but the fact is I take my coffee more seriously than most.

For example, it's the finishing touches, the details, the small things: sweetener and tree milk that were proving so elusive. It would have made the difference as details often do. Was mastering the particulars of coffee preparation really so difficult that even after numerous corrections vociferously shouted whilst stomping my feet high atop my desk, the coffee remained hopeless? Even when I demonstrated the process, a pinch of this, a flair of that, it remained unsatisfactory. I exaggerate, of course, and perhaps I'm making a mountain out of a molehill (that's another of Walter's little beauties—at this point, I'm sure you're catching most of them) but the process confounds me to this day. Why (and how) would he make the coffee so sour?

In the end, I gave in. I got used to it and drank the coffee, warts and all. Maybe I even began to like it. No, I didn't like it, but it made him happy when I pretended to like it. I wanted him to be happy.

—

In my eyes, my father remains two distinct and separate men: one of substance and standing, the other of questionable judgment. The first, and I continue to convince myself more important, is the man who in my youth, took me to the mountains and taught me the survival skills of our ancestors, struggling with me through midnight calculus study sessions, and made me laugh with acts of boundless foolishness. He was the one who dressed as the mischief-maker known as Clown and entertained us with clever antics at birthday celebrations. He's the one who held my five-year-old hand while they applied the first membrane to my trembling skin, skillfully easing my once paralyzing fear. He was the one who forgave me when I drowned our first device in a sink of sea salt and soapy water (he actually told me I helped improve the design). He stood tall, this man, and gave his family priority, even when the stress of the day had worn him thin and all he wanted was to collapse on the living room couch and close his eyes. He's also the man who loved me not, I'm sure, unlike most fathers.

The second man betrayed me from the shadows, perhaps even before the sordid wheels of my conception were in motion. In many ways, he betrayed many of us—all of us. They say it's the quiet ones who are to be most feared, those whose secrets remain intact, unscathed as their last breath is squeezed from withering lungs. My father was such a man and one I had to shake out of the curtains to see clearer. Yet no amount of shaking, no streaming daylight through the window, could truly reveal him. He was the vile one who deftly navigated the ladder of perceived importance even when I repeatedly greased the rungs.

Although I've tried, I can neither combine the competing personas in my memory nor morph them into a more palatable whole. I also cannot release one or the other as separate beings, individuals cleaved down the middle with chisel and hammer or a crack of lightening thrown earthward by a pagan god (I've spent my life attempting this parlor trick). Joining them together, mixing the best of "this" with the not-so-bad of "that" has proven equally fruitless. If given the opportunity, I would cling to the loving father and let the light-hearted Clown triumph while the deceitful one, smote by my still trembling, clenched fist, faded into oblivion. I imagine many would do the same. I try each day in this life, especially since he passed, but forgiveness remains elusive and I remain the more stubborn of the sisters.

It's obvious and clear my parents (all those who can be called parents) arrived, but how was it my parents birthed two children? Or, more accurately, four. And why was it they kept me and offered Barbara as a dowry? Their life, life in the past, seemed so much simpler. It always appears this way when we look at time before we existed, and having not lived in that moment, we simply assume it. People seemed more apt to do what they pleased or what pleased them. If there was a recent time of freedom, it was during my parents' prime, when their muscles and organs and thinking was sound and strong. At least, that's how I envision it. Clearly, those corpulent days of excess are long over.

I'd wondered this about my parents a hundred times as I took to my usual place—my chair on questionable footing in the backyard, formerly the backyard of my parents, the grass wetting my bare feet, the night sky clear, waiting (and willing?) to reveal secrets. It was always my thinking spot…

my dreaming spot. Lately, it was my questioning spot. Was their life so easy as to expect to arrive twice? Just because it's possible, doesn't mean it's possible now. Because we rightly believe we've missed out on something, the pathetic like me always being morbidly curious.

I found the courage to ask my father this question one night as we camped under the stars. I was much older, and we treated our rides into the mountains as much like holidays with a friend as father and daughter. At least that's how I thought of it. A holiday with one of my fathers. But which one?

How was it they raised two children? How was it they birthed four?

He'd shot a quail that afternoon and after an hour digging out gray flecks of birdshot with small metal tweezers and infinite patience, it was cooked slowly over the camp fire. It was a soft fire that glowed pink and orange, one of my finer works…handsome and efficient. It was one that made me proud.

"It was a different time, Talis," he said in response to the question he'd done his best to ignore. "I'm not sure what else I can say." To me, his words were dismissive and stark, a simple answer for a simple-minded daughter who asked a complicated question. His answer was an unemotional shrug of the shoulders, a stoic "just because." I watched his face, greying whiskers and dark circles beneath his eyes, the orange light of the fire unwilling to disguise him.

And that was it—he'd morphed into the second father before my eyes—before dinner was served.

"They were building an army…*raising* an army is a better description, and two children were allowed. It meant two soldiers. That was the only reason." His face remained calm, fatherly even, but his eyes were sad, disappointed. Disappointed in me.

I considered our relationship to be reasonably strong, stronger than most and to continue to press the question, clearly an uncomfortable question for him, could put it at risk. Yet I pressed. I wanted to make him uncomfortable.

"When it was our time, when you had influence, why did you choose Anna over me?"

"I didn't choose her over you," he said.

"You made a choice, right?"

"I did, yes."

"And she was your choice."

"Yes, but not in the way you're thinking."

"Can you explain it to me then? I'd be curious to hear."

He exhaled deeply through his nose, a boisterous, grunting exhale that released more air than was possible for one breath. He was breaking small sticks, twigs for the fire and, for a moment, I felt his strength, his anger perhaps, in the deliberate snap of each one, like he was breaking tiny bones, my tiny bones.

"I'm sorry," he said finally. "I had to make a choice. She was older and I was scared if I didn't raise her name as the choice, place her application in the queue, there may not be another opportunity. What if the next time the list was full and there would be no others? We couldn't risk it. I couldn't risk it."

I listened.

"We, your mother and I, were terrified. One was better than none." He paused. "Of course, two would be wonderful, but that was unlikely." He looked toward me, and softly said, "unlikely."

"I'm sorry," I said and I was. I'd hurt him.

"You don't need to be sorry. You were right to ask, I would have asked if I were you. I should have told you. No, it isn't fair. It wasn't meant to be fair, that's not how the device works."

"No, it's not fair," I said. "You know that for a few more years they did allow more than one? If you'd waited, maybe…"

"That's easy to say now," he interrupted, his face a sharp, gritty red in the firelight, his body tense and angular, ridged. There would be no further discussion. No words at all. We ate dinner in silence, his arms tight to his side and his body turned slightly away from me. When he was finished, he returned to the tent to read. I was left sitting under the stars, my nose thrust upward and eyes wide and alone with the moon as usual.

I realize now that I did mean to hurt him that night as all of my deviances are purposeful. I wanted more. No matter the reasonableness of his reason, there was nothing he could have said to satiate my hunger as my belly is long swollen from this form of malnutrition. No matter the reply, I remain ill-suited to pliability. After all, he could have waited and placed us both on the list the next time around. I'm still paying for his poor choice. I will forever foot the well-tended tab of an unquenchable drunkard. My line ends because of his poor choice. I want my pound of flesh!

I also envisioned this conversation being more cathartic like a lancing of the hideous, reddened boil I carry high on my shoulder, but it did not bring the relief I was desperate to attain. It was all for naught. I've wandered too far down the path. The knees of my pants are soiled and I am pushing with all my might, but the stone refuses to roll, progress has ceased and there is no forward. All this I know…that this explanation by my father was and is to protect Anna. Had he not protected her enough in one lifetime that his decisions still haunt me from the grave?

The backyard chair, the one I spent so many nights perched upon, so comfortably worn to my ample rear and narrow back, grew uncomfortable. Even the setting of a clear night, was less magical and wonderous. The stars faded and, if possible, pushed themselves further away from me, as if light years upon light years away were no longer far enough and they needed that final arm's length. They held such promise when I was young and I was foolish enough to allow promises of the future—impetuous enough to grant these thoughts residence. I know my own bile attempts to block their light and the moon's reflection, dim it down, and make it slightly translucent like looking through a dense weave of fabric or the heavy purple of a stained-glass window. It's there, the starlight, if you really want to see it, but it takes an effort that I grow more unwilling to put forth. Sometimes it's easier to be angry—a conclusion that every mad scientist and evil-doer of the ancient movie films would no doubt agree. I also avoid looking directly at the moon, forsaking its nourishment. It's something I miss dearly.

I realize Lark feels my sting and warm poison being pumped into his veins, subtle and otherwise, as he's slowly eaten alive. It was never his fault, any of it, but wounds that refuse to heal fester and continue to spew disease even to the innocent. Regardless of intent, those closest to us are always at risk. These days, I don't see much of him, but the tentacles of the man o' war spread far and wide and lurk hidden just below the water's surface.

Perhaps, I too, am two distinct people.

Talis
(Is it 5:30?)

Anna is a cruel thing.

Why would she play her tricks on me? Why torture me further? To what ends? And what does Walter gain from her incantations other than the supple skin and bone of her wicked hand? It was all under the guise of a society's altruism. She knew I would bond with him despite my better judgment, so she watched from afar, high upon her pearled throne, set upon her steep, sturdy cliff of smugness as I drowned below in a seething whirl of my own irrational emotions. I even found myself smiling again, of all things, just as she foresaw. Yes, her plan unfolded with both surgical precision and a caped magician's flair. And for that, and more, she was cruel. Happiness is not charity to be meted out to those with perceived need and an outstretched beggar's paw. Happiness is not to be thrust upon us after hasty manufacture to be packaged and distributed by forces unseen. It must happen because it already exists and we've merely wiped away the dust, cleared the grime off an existing patina. There is no other way. All else is false.

But the thing is, and it causes me great pain to admit this, Walter made me forget and, by extension, Anna made me forget my troubles. It was a fresh start and a chance to ease the old wounds, to stitch them closed so they no longer warmly seeped and to speed whatever healing was due. I fought it for many weeks, allowing myself the comfort of an almost stranger, though it was clear he was not a stranger in the traditional sense or in any sense. I knew his voice, his tendencies, his fears, the lines of his body, where everything was located. While I wasn't seeking comfort, there was comfort in it. It was like meeting your first love again but with the slate wiped clean.

However, there was something about Walter other than his odd mannerisms and windy phrases and the way he chewed with is mouth open that was different. Since, to this point, a respectful, comfortable distance was both necessary and mandatory, I hadn't the opportunity to note it. Not only was a respectful and comfortable distance a focal point of Training Pod 7's sanctimoniousness, the fact remained I was a married woman. I kept forgetting. However, along the way, I'd discovered these Echoes, these soldiers, have a lust for life that we sorely lack...a presence, an in-the-moment we've lost somewhere in our accelerated evolution. They respect the ticking clock, the finiteness of existence, the terminal covenant with nature. In our quest for perfection, we've accomplished homogeny and misplaced our humanity, while our reasons for living have lost urgency and sheen.

Scent is not something we've refined or not refined, depending on your perspective. Our ancestors were much keener to this sense, perhaps out of necessity and survival. They sprayed colognes and perfumes to mask stewing unpleasantness, scrubbed with shampoos and soaps and chamois, stripped off the scent of natural oils along with whatever other offenses bubbled to the surface. We tend to not perspire, either—one of the membrane's hidden benefits—preventing us from stinking, wallowing in our filth, and offending a nosey neighbor. I am grateful for it.

I'm told sweat contains urine. Urine! Of all things! What a strange amalgam of body systems to mesh: skin and bladder. It must serve a purpose. Perhaps this was a primal indicator of health one way or another and, therefore, one consideration when choosing a mate. Maybe the available mate with the least offensive odor was front and foremost in the sales pitch. I can hear Delius now, selling me on a potential blind date, the file on the table in front of her festooned with an overly large and recently applied smiley face sticker of approval: "Not only is he housebroken, but he stinks the least of all the tenth-year boys. Hardly a trace of urine on him!"

The point I was about to put forth is, unlike Lark, Walter has a scent. It's a wonderful civet scent. I'm apt to believe it's a scent of good health. It must be because I tend to like it, though I have difficulty describing it. I can say it's pleasant in the same way a pine tree smells pleasant in winter, though he doesn't smell of pine tree or winter. I tend to believe things in nature that are good for us have a scent we find pleasant while things that are dangerous tend to flout a nasal unpleasantness. It's a simplistic and perhaps hopeful theory, no more than a petty rule: things that pass the nose test are deemed good. Things that don't, well, you get the idea. One could argue that Pride was an exception to this rule. You'd find no argument from me.

Walter stood close to me one day in early autumn, physically closer than I'd allowed in our time together. In the earliest days, he was assigned an apartment near Holtsford Park where most of the Echoes were being relocated from temporary housing. Holtsford was the oldest area of the city, run down and slightly sordid, a place where you went to do things you didn't want anyone to know you were doing, and a place where you could procure things you weren't supposed to have.

We stood close enough that day for me to catch his unusual scent. We were waiting for the elevator, a clunking, grinding antique that required you to push buttons and wait for the beast to decide not only whether or not it would lower or raise you to your preferred destination, but whether or not it would even honor you with a squeaking close of the door. As we stood patiently, awaiting its decision on our most recent request, I caught a whiff of him. I leaned a bit toward him and pulled in the unexpected treasure the way I imagine a 19th century miser smelled his ill-begotten money—like it was all mine.

He noticed me leaning in and quietly watched me out of the corner of his eye. He may even have moved closer, ever so slightly, under the guise of adjusting his weight from one foot to the other. When the elevator finally arrived, he waited for me to step in and press the destination floor. Despite room enough for ten people, he stood very close, closer than expected, his hand may have brushed against my thigh.

The one-bedroom apartment was on the eightieth floor and faced the morning sunrise. It was an older building made of swaying, antique carbon fiber girders and windows that no longer effectively filtered UV rays. If scent was to be trusted, the towering apartments of the Holtsford Park area carried humanity's failure conveniently and purposely stuffed into one corner of the world. It smelled unhealthy. Despite its seedy aura and sticky sidewalks, Holtsford Park was close to many of the "trendy" cafes and restaurants—if convenience was a fair trade off for good looks (and brash odors), then the apartment was a swell find.

Walter was elated to have an apartment to himself. He said it was the most space he'd ever had and wasn't sure what he was going to do with it all. Well within my job description, I told him I'd help decorate and get him up to speed, demonstrate the appliances and, of course, the coffee maker. Even in his jubilant state, the first cup he made was disappointing.

A few weeks later, I ran into Delius's Echo in the lobby of the apartment building. She, of course, didn't recognize me. It was a strange interaction, watching someone you know, or should know, ignore you. She held the beauty of Delius, but she carried it even better, like the mold-maker had improved the second time around. Her eyes were the same, a stately mauve, grand and alluring, like her mother had instructed the doctors. She smiled at me, at least I think she did, and said hello to Walter in an unusual manner—flirty, almost mischievous, like someone who knows all your dark secrets. With a wink, she melted into the elevator, the squeaking door squeezing her wry smile. I wanted to stop her, to talk with her, to tell her I knew her…her what? Her real self? The original model? The one her parents chose to keep?

She said something odd that day. Although, it wasn't really what she said that was odd, but the context or lack of context.

Before the door to the elevator closed, as she was waiting for it to seal and separate us from her, she asked Walter in a flirty, familiar voice, "Is it 5:30?"

Walter responded, "Not yet."

I checked the time. It was 6:38 pm.

"Do you know her?" I asked.

"Yes, sort of," he said. "Her name is Harriet. She was under the command of my Sargent-Major."

"Do you speak with her often?"

"No, not really," he said and shrugged his shoulders. "I've seen her here in the lobby a couple of times."

"Strange the way she looked at you."

"Like the cat that ate the canary?" he asked.

"The what?"

"The cat that ate the canary."

I may have looked even more confused than I felt.

"Like she knows something we don't," he explained.

I considered this for a moment. That look, the connection she shared with Walter (was there a wink?), what did it mean? And what about that strange body language, a toss of hair as she slinked into the waiting elevator? Was that a signal or was I looking for veiled meaning where there was none to be found?

"Why did she ask if it was 5:30?"

"Maybe she was curious of the time."

"Wasn't it an odd thing to ask? And why didn't she hold the elevator for us?"

"Don't worry about her. She's mostly harmless," he said warmly and leaned in close to me. I thought he might take my hand in his, here, in a public place. I felt my body stiffen and my eyes widen.

"I'll make you some coffee so you can relax, take a load off," he said.

I told him my stomach was upset, but I didn't say it was because I knew the direction the night was taking and I was growing nervous.

"Nothing soothes the stomach like my coffee," he said with a wink and smile. I never told him about his coffee. I have to believe he was trying his best.

That night, under the ghostly green glow of the device, in a nondescript apartment eighty floors above Holtsford Park, I let him undress me for the first time. Or rather it was the first time we undressed each other. It was slow and pleasant and just right, like we'd rehearsed for a hundred years and made our debut to a sweeping, thunderous applause. I was concerned about my marriage. As Walter would say, I'd really "stepped in it."

As it turns out, that night didn't cause the feared turmoil in my existence or modify the trajectory of my being. The next morning, however, changed everything.

Lark
(The Keys)

Before the troubles, our troubles, Talis loved to holiday. One year, we took a holiday to the Key Islands. Is that what they used to call it—a holiday or was it a vacation? I can't recall. It was during this respite she returned, briefly, to the unburdened, carefree girl I met, bright faced and a slower, though still determined, gait. No, she was never carefree, but she was in balance. She did well to hide her burdens.

At one time, there were 800 keys in Old Florida stretching a hundred miles from the mainland. Now there are 10,000 sundrenched rocks and more on order for each month. More land! Yes, more land to house the growing population. Strip the northern mountains bare, flatten them like pancakes grind them down with excavators and graders, fill in the water, build it up high, plop down weatherproof structures of carbon fiber and glue. Move them in. Don't look back.

The water was glorious…teal and clear as a fresh glass of water, warm and silky to the touch. The beach sand, bleached, processed, and delivered, white as powdered sugar, was soft on the delicate undersides of my feet. And we weren't alone—bare breasted men and woman walked hand in hand along the water, caring little for either the appetites or parochial ways of others. The trees were mangy and filled with yellow and black spiders, absorbing salt and growing sideways (the trees, not the spiders). The rain schedule proved problematic as it called for rain nearly every month, but we were generally able to work our plans around it.

The membrane was rudimentary in those days, more a thin coat of paint than a fully functional layer of protection, and after a day basking in unfiltered sunlight, our skin was pinkish and slightly warm to the touch. At night, the bed grew hot from our radiation "burns," and we didn't sleep much or at all. The device spewed automated warnings concerning our radiation exposure, self-righteous speeches addressing our child-like behavior. It felt like we'd angered Mom and now had to sit through her long overdue speech before we could have dinner. We deserved the device's wrath, though we laughed to ourselves and refused to alter our increasingly deviant habits. If you can't deviate on holiday, then why holiday at all?

One evening after a particularly long day of sunlight exposure, I poked and prodded Talis' arm with my index finger and watched as the small circle of skin briefly turned from a well-earned pink to her completion's olive-white.

"I'm changing before your very eyes," she said as she watched where I pressed with my finger. "I'm a chameleon. Do it again!"

"You'll never change," I said.

"I've already changed."

"That's from the sun, white to pink to white," I said.

"I've changed inside."

We were in love then. Or we thought we were. Or I thought we were. We too, walked hand in hand and gazed into each other's eyes and often peeled off each other's clothes. Is that love? Is that what lovers do? Is it the same thing? I'm too foolish to know for sure and I'm not sure I've ever known. Some people take pride in knowledge and in years of study or experience that provides a well-lit view of things such as enlightenment of life and love. I'm not one of those people.

We spent eight weeks on a key, a rock surrounded by malignant blue and green water rippling, cresting, always in motion but never reaching a destination. Magnificent. We ate meals meant for a dozen, stuffed ourselves blue with proteins we'd never experienced: pink shrimp, grilled lion-fish, broiled manatee, and spiced sea turtle. We requested the device not alarm us to the approaching morning, and we spent hours alone under sheets made of cotton, hemp and pine bark minding our burns and fulfilling our physical impulses. Most importantly, for sixty days we forgot who we were and what it meant to be us. The bad us. The unfortunate us. The ignorant us. The ones judged each new year by a faceless tyrant crunching and whittling obtuse numbers until they're razor sharp before cutting us raw.

We swam too, in the ocean of all places! Or was it a gulf or a bay? I can't say for sure, but within it, whatever it was, we swam and frolicked and generally made fools of ourselves. Neither of us was a swimmer which is to say neither of us was raised to be swimmers who swam. We, the both of us, sort of bobbed in the saltwater, listing to one side or another, before righting ourselves by thrusting our feet into the sand and rocks and broken shells that populated the bottom of the ocean or the gulf or the bay. I lost count of how many cuts I received on my toes and feet, victims of the rocks and shells and perpetually soft living. One of the better thought out, secondary purposes of the membrane was to serve as a floatation device, or at least a not drowning device. To this challenge, the performance was questionable, but the fact we remained above the surface of the water speaks to the general robustness of the feature.

We were quite a sight, two barely buoyant pinkish, terrestrial mammals wrestling in the warm surf, cleaving to the surface with arms chopping and legs kicking. There was laughing, there must have been, as we lolled in the water, asking aloud who was more likely to tire and succumb to the elements. Water is an enigma and a purveyor of both life and death, and on this holiday, it was a modicum of long overdue entertainment.

I yelled "Shark!" several times over the course of eight weeks and watched Talis scramble, screaming at the top of her lungs, arms cutting through the warm air, her legs attempting to run through the seawater, her knees pumping, struggling through the heaviness of the brine. I bobbed loosely not more than a few feet away, quite calm despite my shrieks of alarm. There, of course, were no sharks.

They're fables relegated to the pages of children's books and graduate studies. They'd long ago joined the dodos and the elephants and the honeybees—ghosts that haunt our sleep but little else.

I thought it amusing to have a laugh at her expense. She thought me immature.

It was a fair assessment on her part. When the warning of "shark!" had lost its appeal, I resorted to more creative, if not crueler tactics—tugging at the small of her ankle, dragging her lower until her mouth filled with warm brine and fish piss. She kicked and flung her arms like we were wrestling again, choking on the salt as it filled her nose and mouth. The sharp edges of her fingernails dragged along my arms and the blunt rump of her heel smashed against my shin leaving me scratched and bruised but undeterred. Apparently, she didn't share my opinion that it was humorous to purposely fill someone with the fear of drowning. It was the first time I'd seen her cry. Upon reflection, I sought a reaction from her…something, anything…even something negative, to make me feel like she noticed me. Like I was important again.

"You're an asshole!" she bellowed once free from my grasp and made her way toward the shore. And I was that ancient moniker and the unpleasant exit it represented, if only for the moment. It couldn't have been enjoyable for her, my constant needling and the threats of attack, an annoying pull of an ankle or splash of water that wet her face and stung her eyes. Yet, to me, this toying with another all seemed natural, almost a rite of passage. Again, wasn't it what lovers do, the soft, playful underbelly of being a couple? Wasn't this how they found their place? Wasn't this flirtatious subterfuge?

I was young and foolish to the ways of the world (am I still foolish at least?), though now the muddied moment in time is less murky—it was Talis who was growing wiser by the day. In the early days, she carried heavier burdens than I. Did she suspect, despite our hopes and society's words of encouragement, we would never arrive? Did she know I was also drawn to Delius, making our bond weaker in the process? The slow crawl of time would suggest she did.

The memories of our time in the sun, even now, remain remarkably unscathed; they remain, at worst and despite my aberrant behavior, amiable. I hope to carry their goodwill with me, sneaking them past whatever unpleasantness lies in wait—a thief smuggling an ounce of holy water out of the church.

On that same trip, the holiday-vacation, I commissioned a bracelet for Talis—one that held the implication of impending motherhood. It was called, fittingly, an "Arrival" bracelet, and they were quite trendy at the time. The name was a clever marketing ploy to be sure, but it was one that allowed me to communicate my hope without fear of fumbled or hollow words. It was made of roped rare metals mined on Mars and interwoven with the finest lunar copper and red flax. It was lighter than air and glowed reddish in the daylight. My metal selections worked together seamlessly (or at least I like to think so). It was stunning.

I commissioned one of the local artisans to weave it for

me (they were famous for it at the time), and it was ready in a week. The jeweler was tall and slender with pale skin pulled tightly over her face and she spoke with a professor's sagely confidence. Her hair was unusually long, most way down her back, and blond, brown, mauve, orange and green, like she was all things or embraced change like afternoon winds. Her eyes, too, were odd and eclectic—one was blue as the sky, the other, brownish-green like a field in late summer. In her profession, at least, it was best to be a chameleon.

"This design is specifically for expected arrivals, time-less, yes?" she asked in a soft voice while smiling for the first time. Her teeth were small and square, arranged like a per-fect row of fencing, and a dull white, the sheen worn down by time and salt air. The pink of her gums was slightly visible where her lips were stretched. I nodded along in agreement. What else could I do?

"It's good luck to wear it, of course," she said while admiring her work from different angles, lifting the bracelet higher then lower, turning her head, using the blue, then brownish-green eye in an ad-hoc quality study. "Are you arriving soon?"

"Yes," I said quickly as my nerve began to slip, my voice fading. "It should be this year. Or soon."

How could I know?

I hadn't expected to feel the pressure the bracelet or even the thought of the bracelet would form in my gut. Sour bile began to rise from my stomach and my throat burned. What had I done? What an arrogant fool I'd become!

"This will make a fine gift, something that will be passed

down for generations," she said and nodded her approval of my selection of metals. I had little choice in the matter, as she had guided me along, clawing at my shirt collar until the decisions were firm.

"These reddish strands represent a long and prosperous life," she continued, using a bony finger to trace along the surface of the bracelet. She'd begun her sales presentation even though I was already committed to the purchase. It would have been a better use of our collective time to save the speech for someone in need of convincing.

"These are mined robotically near the equator of Mars, deep toward the center of the planet. The ore is melted down and, as it cools, twisted into rope, like you see here. Quite rare and wonderful." Whether she was telling the truth about the metals place of origin or not, I can't say. It's entirely possible it was dug from under the very earth I stood upon.

"I'm sorry, I've forgotten to offer my congratulations," she said with a little bow of her head, her varied hair falling full over her face, hiding her eyes behind a curtain of mauve, orange and green. "Have you made your selections on the child?" she asked though I sensed her interest had waned. "You look like yellow eyes would be a preference."

"Thank you," I replied. "Not yet, no. Those details are best left to my wife."

"Yes," she said and looked through me like I'd offered my goodbye an hour earlier or she finally realized I was a lost cause. I don't know which it was. "If you lack conviction in it, that would be best."

Yes, I remained committed to the act: the thought, the research, the design, the purchase and now, *now* the final falling upon the sword. I'd see it through. But all this wasn't due to my concern over our future, Talis' and mine; it was strictly an accounting of time. I knew, or thought at the time, we were meant to arrive at some point, were destined even, if such a thing exists and one could have a destiny to follow. Slowly, I regained whatever composure I'd held prior to this sallow bout of anxiety. A good deed, yes! That's what it was. My shoulders straightened and my spine flattened. The jeweler looked at me out of the corner of her eyes, sensing my epiphany. I now held all the intentions and undue confidence of the righteous. Nothing could stop me. The bracelet fit into a flat, circular container I placed in my back pocket.

We'd had an agreeable night, dinner on a pier that reached a half-mile out over the water. There were numerous restaurants and entertainment venues built on the wide planks—I'd chosen one from a brochure retrieved from the device at the hotel. The weather was typical for the winter season and during the evening hours was a reasonably pleasant, one-hundred-ten degrees.

We ordered a local favorite, Chowder of Conch. That much I remember, but not much more as the evening took an unexpected and unfortunate turn.

We were seated near a railing almost at the end of the

pier. It was mostly silent other than the drone of windmills, voices of diners enjoying their evening and soft, angelic music emanating from the piano where a bearded gentleman was deftly working the keys between sips of wine. I'd ordered a bottle of absinthe, warmed in a bath of water and two glasses.

"We don't drink," Talis said to me in a slinky, provocative manner after I'd ordered and the waiter had wandered off. There was a tinny suspicion in her voice, but she was ready to listen to whatever speech I'd prepared.

"It's a special occasion," I assured her with a smile.

"Oh?"

"It is."

"And what occasion might it be?" She asked and returned the smile. I'd piqued her interest.

She had a wonderful smile then when we were young. It surely remains today, but long ago I ceased to be the recipient of its delightfulness. I'm not sure she'd say the same of me, that I had a wonderful smile, as I was not one to smile often. I always found it unnatural and insincere, perhaps because I usually felt as much each time I hammered one across the width of my face. A lovely polished smile, like the one Talis wore early that evening, was always beyond my ability to conjure. It took practice and a certain charm to mean it.

A warm wind carried in a scent of saltiness and decay, not an unpleasant smell, mind you, but one that was unfamiliar and demanding of attention. We both pulled it in through our noses and looked at each other and laughed—

the contortions our faces had made at the odd and certainly unexpected odor made us snort and carry-on like…like us.

The absinthe arrived, warmed to perfection, and the waiter poured two glasses halfway full. The moon, almost full and reflecting the light of the unseen sun, provided the evening a blanket of soft gray light and the liquid glowed a fine mint green. We each raised a glass, the warmth pleasant in my hand. I brought the glass to my lips and felt the liquid, thick as syrup, slide down my throat.

"The moon makes me foolish," she said as she stared upward, taking in the light like it was warming her face. "It makes me dream, but it's fading."

"The moon is fading?"

"No," she said and shook her head like I was impossible and never understood. "The dream."

"I don't have dreams," I said, only half joking. "I'm incapable of them. It's one of my many charms."

I expected a quick rebuke, a stern lecture about what my dreams might be, according to Talis, and how I need to follow them until they were either achieved or no more. But I was met with silence and salt air and moonlight and the soft notes of piano. She was staring upward, dreaming, as usual. I reached into my back pocket and slid the circular container across the table.

She was guarded from the start and fingered the container without any attempt to open it, sliding it around the table like it was greased and she was unable to grasp it. She poked at it with her index finger as if it were a gag gift, an old-time springy snake stuffed into a canister waiting to scare the unsuspecting. I fought the urge to encourage her, to guide her along to my ends. Eventually, she peeled the top with the tips of her fingers, prying open the cover a sliver, attempting to sneak up on whatever hid inside. Curiosity, though, is a crafty mistress…and it was to curiosity, and nothing else, she succumbed.

"Do you even know what this is?" she asked when she set eyes on the bracelet, her voice tight and rough like she'd been exposed to a potent allergen. "It's something you give when someone is about to arrive!"

"Yes, but I just thought…"

Despite her displeasure, she remained calm, detached from the moment, like a balloon that's broken away and floats free, alone, to its doom. The slight, however unintended, provided a moment of introspection and she stared skyward toward that invisible balloon as it rose toward oblivion, toward the moon and its empty promises.

"I may never arrive," she said while scooping the bracelet from the container. She turned in over in her hand, inspecting it, trying to find a reason to want it. The muscles of her arm grew taut and twitched like they were planning something, before she tossed the bracelet high into the air, over the railing of the pier and into the ocean or the gulf or the bay and was done with it.

"I don't deserve to have it," she said.

I watched the reddish metal spinning as it hurled through the air, catching a small glint of moonlight, a brief sparkle, before it dove out of sight without a sound. Much later, when I thought of the bracelet (and I have thought of it often), I wondered if in that small glint of moonlight, the bracelet that sits in a watery grave, the one which represented the dreams of so many, had dreams of its own crushed that evening. Did it have a purpose in being made? Or was it representative of something else entirely, a flash, a brief fiery moment which scorched a future beyond recognition?

The moment it disappeared on the other side of the railing, my face and my body turned toward Talis, my mouth hung open without doubt, my good deed gone horribly wrong. It wasn't the expense of it that rattled me, though it was certainly a factor, it was the thoroughness in which she decried the gesture, the confidence in which she wielded authority. She of no hope held all the power.

"You're a fool, Lark! Don't give me hope," she said.

And I never did again. That was that. I was too afraid to tell her, too much the coward to say, the whole gambit, the entire idea, was because I still held hope. What would be the point?

Until that moment, I hadn't considered failure. Our relationship would slowly deteriorate and succumb to the decay of time. It likely had already commenced, but it was the first time I took notice. It was, thankfully, a slow process that didn't manifest itself day to day but rather year to year, spanning a decade, maybe two. There are some who expect and hope their demise will be swift and painless, but a demise of this nature, one of the heart with so much invested, is better to work at such sloth-like pace to remain undetected. It's my preference to never detect it at all, ever the ostrich with his head in the sand.

On that same holiday, the one of the failed gift—the bracelet that would not bring happiness—Talis bought a sweater for me or, rather, had acquired one prior to the trip and hidden it away within her luggage. When she presented it to me, she did not mention the bracelet or even, as I may have, attempted a joke to break the thickening ice. It was about a week later, maybe two weeks, so it's possible she'd moved past our awkward ordeal.

Oddly, it wasn't a new sweater but an old vintage model, forest green and white with a touch of red, thick wool yarn with knitted patterns of trees and mountains. The sleeve elbows were slightly worn and shiny, thinner than the rest and the cuffs and collar were just beginning to fray. The wool itself smelled like outside, slightly wild and musty, yet familiar, like a traditional song sung slightly off-key by the warmth of a campfire. In giving it, the sweater seemed so much more to Talis than a simple garment—it carried the weight of history. This I could tell by her face, warmer than usual, slightly pinkish, her mouth elongated into a wry, crooked smile. Had the sweater belonged to her father? Had he worn it on their oft-told adventures into the mountains? Did it bear witness to the legendary people of the mountains? If so, why would she gift it to me?

Certainly, the sweater was something I could wear on a trip to the mountains. Was this a gesture of healing after the bracelet had gone so wrong? She didn't say. I was too stunned to ask, expecting the moment to implode and find myself running for a yet to be determined exit. While I did intend to wear the sweater on at least one trip to the mountains, presumably to recreate the trips she made with her father, the trip itself never materialized. The gesture, given time, proved as hollow as the bracelet.

Talis
(Sharkskin Soap)

I'd spent the night in Holtsford Park, something I couldn't have imagined only a few weeks earlier. And I'd spent the night sniffing him—yes, sniffing—taking in this wonderful new scent that made me weak and pliable, and I admit, available. How modern a woman I'd become. What a peculiar turn of events. What a peculiar thing to enjoy. Is it love when something expectedly repulsive becomes tolerable or even desirable? Or is it the curse of joy?

As I sniffed and snorted, he wore a concerned look on his face, his eyes squinted and nose crunched upward like he'd eaten a lemon and wasn't sure if he was supposed to enjoy or not. This look told me he was wondering what it was, exactly, I was doing. I buried my cold nose here and there: in the pit of his arm, deep into the pale skin of his neck, down into…well, you get the idea, but he was either too polite to ask, or was allowing himself to enjoy it. Or, more likely, he sensed I was enjoying myself and didn't want to be a heel.

A heel. The Echo's odd use of language is rubbing off on me, those ancient and extinct phrases come in handy like Walter said they would. What was this manner, really, trapped in time and slave to pre-modernism?

For an evening, I forgot about my life, my regrets and expectations…the lot of it. I forgot about Anna and her perfect little arrival and my father and his deceit and Lark and how we used to finish each other's thoughts. In an instant, my existential rift was bridged and rendered moot, unimportant. It was just him and me and whatever scents we were conjuring together, whatever pheromones we released into the air in fits and starts. It was just us, our eyes and our bodies and our lust.

Until I called him "Lark."

Although he laughed softly and dismissed of my gaffe, my skin began to burn, then itch. I was trapped inside my body with no escape. Even the membrane did not ease this pimply outbreak of skin discomfort—it was poison ivy all over again. Was the malignant sting of hornets, the piercing delivery of their throbbing stinger and pumping poison soon to follow? The moment, for it was only a moment before he spoke, was a hundred years of torture.

"I know who your husband is," he said with a boyish, embarrassed grin and his face began to pink in the cheeks. "I know everything about him. It's my job to know."

"Do you know what he'd say if he knew we spent this night together?" I asked.

"I don't know him that well," he said and laughed. Not surprisingly, Walter possessed many familiar, endearing qualities, but for the first time I noticed he had Lark's wonderful laugh.

—

I had official access to the records of my Echoes, the ones under my direct care, but was unable to research the mysterious Harriet masquerading as Delius. It was one of the unfortunate realities of privacy law and the device, for all its faults, was a notorious stickler for privacy. I wanted to research her strange phrase, her question: 'Is it 5:30?' I couldn't get it out of my head and like many worries, I took it to bed with me, let it stew and simmer, hoping it would tenderize under the pressure of a slow cook. Why would someone ask a relative stranger about a time that held no apparent relevance? She had to know it was after 6:30 or at least known 5:30 had already passed. Which, of course, meant it was relevant.

After borrowing Anna's device access (a dismissible offense, yes), I was able to uncover some history of this phrase. As best I could discern, it was a derivative of popular slang from the twentieth century, a phrase used by Mid-Levs and office clerks to infer they were awaiting the end of the workday so they could meet at the local public house for alcoholic beverages. It indicated and encouraged a friendly, social gathering after hours meant to build cohesive relationships amongst office workers of the age. Actually, the phrase I uncovered was more relevant to "5 o'clock," but I assumed it was an offshoot.

So, what did this mean in terms of Harriet? I can only conclude this was an attempt to flirt with Walter, to gather his attention to her. He was after all, a free man who was being integrated into society. On the official record, he was officially available. Perhaps she was inviting him for a drink with hopes of encouraging the very amorous activities I was currently enjoying.

With Anna's access, I could have done deeper research on Harriet, gleaned her little secrets, her weaknesses, muddied my hands, but this may have brought undue scrutiny on Anna—and soon after to me. There was little need take my rogue research further once I had the secret of Harriet's flirtatious "5:30." Taking it further risked a red-light on the device…something I was loathe to trigger.

———

Why were Echoes taught extinct jargon? When designing a program, it's important to have fail-safes—ways to identify and rectify problems in quick, simple ways. This vernacular was one of the fail-safes for the Echo program, a relatively simple way for the Intelligence Office to identify an Echo if they met one on the street. Anna, unsurprisingly, had access to all the secrets and I learned as many as I could.

Another fail-safe was the lack of membranes. Their skin's dull, flat finish was fairly easy to identify once you knew the characteristics. For the fair-skinned Echoes, like Walter, they often carried a pinkish hue when exposed to the sun or when they heated from exertion. That first evening in the

Holtsford apartment, Walter grew lobster red and heated, emitting steam and perspiration that smelled like evolution itself was at work. I didn't mind.

That same first evening I also discovered the scars on his back, deep ruts of damaged flesh forming ridges and valleys from shoulder to buttocks, healed tissue thickened like tortoise shell. Though perhaps not an intended fail-safe, these scars were both the result of punishment and a sign of respect earned under unpleasant conditions. They could not be mistaken for anything else.

"How did this happen?" I asked one evening (though not the first) as we lay in a warm bed eighty floors up.

"What do you do when you want to teach someone to obey without hesitation?" he asked softly, but with the confidence of a true believer.

"I don't know," I said.

"You teach them that to not obey will cause more pain than obeying," he explained. "Elegant. Simple, really."

"It sounds cruel."

He reflected upon it for a moment, squinting his eyes and exhaling a long, warm gust of air through his nose.

"Cruelty is sending one twin into battle while the other is fat from dinner and drink and sleeps soundly in a warm bed, free from worry because another is on watch," he said. "Once you accept that little cruelty, the rest is easy."

His response was matter-of-fact, like he was resigned to this fate. It was a shrug of the shoulder, another day. He held no apparent anger at his station.

"Did you kill anyone?" The words slid from the corner

of my mouth before I had a chance to smother them back into my cheek. Did I come across as equally matter-of-fact?

"Yes," he said rather shyly (if it was possible to answer this question and remain shy) and raised a hand up to scratch his ear. "That was the job I was created to do. When we are at war, things are different. When the device gives you an assignment, you must follow it." Despite his willingness to answer my question, I don't believe he meant his initial commentary to lead to this acknowledgement and confirmation.

"I'm sorry," I said. "I shouldn't pry." Had I embarrassed him?

At this, he looked at me like he was receiving a usual punishment, one he'd grown accustomed to being meted out in his presence, a switch swung to the formally delicate flesh of the back. We began the day as equals and now he was staring up at me. I felt foolish.

It'd been decades since anyone was murdered in open society. I'd never met anyone who'd killed another or heard of someone who'd met someone. No one had. Then again, I'd met Harriet, and she was of similar stock and I'm sure the scaly skin of her back would verify her guilt. She looked devious enough to take a life though I'm sure Delius would be unsettled by this observation.

And what of my assault on Anna? Would this crime qualify me for Harriet's lofty, deviant status? Would it make me a killer who lacked follow through? A savage who lost conviction? A half-way? A coward? I must remember to reserve judgment. After all, I was willing to provide Walter a pass.

"It's different now," he said. "Everything is different now. Our lives have changed."

And it was true, everything was different…even more than I knew. In the next hours, it would be irreversibly confirmed.

—

The bathroom, like the rest of the apartment, was modest, primitive, lost in time, even before the time of my great-grandmother and sorely lacking the charming color scheme of her tasteful eye. It was stark white, tiled from floor to ceiling as if it foresaw its future and almost institutional purpose. The only contrast in the room was the dull, powder blue of the shower stall and the tone of my skin, the blue of my eyes staring back from the dulled mirror.

Hairline cracks in the aging, powder blue shower tiles ran in every direction, like the wrinkles of aged and neglected skin before the invention of the membrane. The shower drain reeked of swamp and spoiled runoff and proudly wore a gritty, greenish tinge. The rusty, manual fixtures squeaked open and shut, requiring a steady hand to produce a measured mix of hot and cold water. I spent several minutes attempting to balance the temperature, too hot, then too cold, never just right. It seemed such a waste of time, testing the water, making adjustments and testing the adjustments. Even worse, I soaked my arm up to the shoulder in cold or tepid or scalding water each time I was forced to reach into that baleful stall to make the next valve adjustment.

A small, rectangular shelf in the corner of the stall held a slightly smaller, rectangular bar of soap, blue, like the tiles, but rough to the touch, like the skin of the extinct shark I'd touched at a museum. Not coincidentally, there was a silhouette of a shark embossed onto the bar itself. On an earlier occasion, I'd asked Walter about this strange soap, so odd to the eye, unusual to the touch.

"It's used to scrub stuff," he said.

"It's soap, so I assumed it's used for scrubbing."

"For blood."

"What?"

He laughed in that pale way shy men interact with the world. He didn't make eye contact. "Every soldier has a need for it sooner or later. It's not as clean a job as…whatever it is you do, wherever you hang your hat."

I didn't press the question further. I didn't want to know about the blood.

While adjusting the valves one way or the other, I became light-headed, and when I looked down at my feet, I was dizzy and slightly off-balance. A dark rim formed in my peripheral vision; the aperture closed to nearly pitch black before opening slowly. I held the wall to keep steady. My feet looked pale and fragile, almost ghostly on the cold tile, the highway of thin blue veins barely contrasting the white floor. They itched. Over the last couple of days, my breasts had grown increasingly sore and tender to the touch. I'd recently developed a pain deep in my abdomen with no obvious source.

The hot water (finally, I'd made the requisite adjustments)

was steaming the mirrors and dampening the walls, forming small beads of water on the white tile. Expanding clouds of steam muffled the light, rendering it translucent and unreliable as I slipped off my underwear. They dropped to the floor and, as I'd done ten thousand times before, I stepped out of them. When I looked down to pick them up, I didn't believe my eyes. Was the steam and failing light playing its tricks? I screamed. Walter didn't seem to hear. I was still alone.

There was blood, deep crimson and heavy, staining the fabric of my underwear and swirled down the length of my thigh. I hadn't sustained an injury. It could only be one thing: an internal hemorrhage.

No. Not a hemorrhage.

It carried all the signs of everything I'd read—the stories of those luckier than myself.

It.

But how could this be possible? My legs no longer supported the weight of my body, no longer answered to me. I knelt on the bathroom floor for several minutes, the billowing steam warming my back.

In a moment of clarity, however brief, I was glad for the blue, sharkskin soap.

Lark
(Home)

What happens when home no longer feels like home? And what happens when absinthe no longer provides comfort, no longer nourishes the soul? This is what I was left to consider. Or rather, what was left of me—all the foolish questions a man can muster. It was a hollowness, a sense of being nowhere despite being somewhere familiar. Now, I was somewhere formally familiar. That sounds foolish even to me. There were two places I comfortably existed: home and under the ever-changing spell of absinthe. Now, they remained, but had changed, morphed, broken and reformed like a gold family heirloom melted and reclaimed in a crucible then poured into a new, unexpected mold.

There were still brief visits "home" to the bed I shared with Talis for decades. I'm not sure what I expected to find or how I expected to feel. It may not be home to Talis either, at least when I'm beside her, but I can't speak for her. She's cold and distant, a stranger striding alongside a stranger, the repulsed sprawled beside the repulsive. Who can blame her?

In another life, a former life it seems now, our bodies kept each other warm at night, limbs intertwined, vining along our length, effortlessly becoming one. Often our lips met in the night, salty and warm, at times salty and warm from the tears sliding down her cooled cheek, spilling over the sharp ridges of her golden lips. When she was sad, I was sad, too. Or at least sadness is what we always had in common. At least toward the end.

Our shared meals, when times were good, were effortless, conversations fruitful and filled with insight. It was natural, easy. I enjoyed it so, all of it. But are my recollections tainted by time, fogged by a perceived happiness that didn't exist other than in my hopeful memories? Time is not a fickle forgiver—it's the great healer. Take it all away. I'm aware the end grows nearer. Now my life is in flashing review.

Talis liked to spend time alone in her garden. That's what she called it: her "garden," a ramshackle greenhouse she and her father raised in the backyard (the eyesore of the neighborhood). It reeked of mud and dust and honest hope. The hours spent watering this and pruning that was when she was happiest, seemed happiest at least, as I never could tell for sure. Over the measure of a week, it was her sanctuary, a delirious escape from her menacing reality. Perhaps it was also an escape from me. I hadn't considered it until now.

Often, at dusk, I watched her from the kitchen window. I'd press my face up against the cool glass, watching her silhouette, alternately still as night and hustling about like a storm was approaching an ill-prepared farm and she was the last line of defense for all its creatures. It was lovely watching her work. She moved in smooth, dignified transitions, her caretaking choreographed for a ballerina. Such was the weight she carried to my eyes. At least for a time.

I wonder if she knew my voyeuristic tendencies in my gawking, studying the lines of her body, the way she moved in the fading evening light, yellow rubber gloves pulled high on her forearms and a great straw hat atop her head. The hat, of course, was made redundant by the membrane, yet somehow it remained an integral accessory while also a flattering addition. I should have told her I'd been watching from the window and that I found myself unable to look away. I should have told her how beautiful she was, and how proud of her I was, but words were never my dearest friends.

When I did speak, it was always something clumsy and juvenile, something that never helped my cause. I used to tease that she was having an affair in that filthy, rustic orchard, intercourse under the translucent, weather-beaten glass. Yes, there, amongst the peppers and tomatoes, the apples and cranberries, her clothing stained with soil and fertilizer. Those same clothes were stripped off and left in an unkempt pile on the floor, her olive skin streaked with pollen, rolling about with someone who wasn't me.

What made me think such a vile thing? What reason? I did wonder—is there something about being so close to nature that draws upon our ancient lack of sensibilities? Are there some long-lost instincts that are enticed and magnified, set forth by the sweet scent of nature that encourages debauchery and donnybrooks?

Donnybrook. That's one of Harriet's long out of use words, and I must confess I have no idea if I've used it correctly. Or if it's even a word. She presented that one to me while describing our wrestling and copulating. Or perhaps we were copulating and wrestling. I'm not sure if it matters, but it was part of her description of our adulterous maneuverings one morning in early autumn. It was all part of her enigmatic charm and a unique ability to conjure happiness and confusion in the same breath.

Many times, I meant to tell Talis about Harriet—to confess my sexual donnybrook—but, to no one's surprise, I proved the coward.

There was another concern. It was more introspective and, in many ways, more frightening. Many of my fondest memories of Talis, good memories (and even some not so good), solid and meaningful, were being slowly usurped by new memories made with Harriet. Unlike many of the memories of the recent past, these new memories were happier, more carefree, unclouded by "what ifs," or veiled under the long shadow of arrival. Should I feel guilty for these indulgences? Was this moment of unencumbered bliss simply wrong, or were they the natural result of our station being sheared and torn clean through? And, in a larger sense, was the pressure of society strangling us with our own expectations? In other words, was escape the logical or even preferred outcome? Was it inevitable?

What would become of Talis and me? What would become of Harriet and me?

I already knew. Harriet told me. She told me everything.

Lark
(Neville)

One morning, Harriet and I embarked on a hike, the old-fashioned activity I'd often read about. I hired a transport to take us out of the city and west toward the mountains. How far we traveled is difficult to say, but an hour later, we arrived at the location I'd read about in a glossy. There was a trail mapped and coded, twisting to the top of a mountain, ready for our exploration.

I'd procured appropriate clothing from the purser in the basement of a building in Holtsford. It was the place you went when you didn't want anyone to know what you were purchasing, and purchasing mountain survival suits was not something you wanted to broadcast. Anna was kind enough to recommend such a place, one where every transaction was discreet. I was careful to not confess my leisure activities to Anna and, surprisingly, she didn't ask. For all Anna's perceived penchant for the law, her straight neck and back, and her clean fingernails, she was quite knowledgeable in the darker arts.

The purser himself was a wisp of a man with brownish eyes, an elongated face like a buoy and full lips that ran across from ear to ear. He looked the part of an error, a mistake, a cookie not fully baked or dough dropped on the floor before being rescued and tossed back onto the pan. He was not one of the perfect specimens I was used to seeing above ground, and that may be how he found his way down to the basement level and the seedy, black-market business. I felt bad, at least a little, making such a judgment about Neville—that was his name—as if my own baking had produced only fine desserts and little else, instead of an empty pan.

Neville was an Echo; I know because he told me. And, to use one of Harriet's endearments, he "stuck out like a sore thumb."

Neville's "office," as he called it, was little more than a refurbished counter from an antique diner with a greenish-marble top and two padded, swiveling stools bolted to the floor, one on either side of the counter. The countertop was worn from use, the top finish shorn white from sliding this or that across from Neville (and likely his predecessors) to his nervous clientele.

There were three gray, metal lights, possibly fission power types, hanging down from the ceiling by cords or cables. They dangled a few feet above the counter, swinging gently back and forth, moved by a nonexistent breeze. They provided the dim basement with an odd, whitish glow, like we were on a spot-lit theater stage and the silent audience was hidden behind a curtain of darkness. By pointing his thumb (how odd), Neville directed me to sit on the swiveling stool bolted on my side of the counter. The heat from the middle light began to burn a hole in the top of my head, so I leaned my body backward and rested my hands on the counter in front of me. He looked at me with squinted eyes, like he was wondering if I found his scent offensive and was placing some needed space between us. It's possible I had and did.

He held two green suits in his springy arms and sized me up before placing them on the counter. The suits were thick and rubbery but soft to the touch. There were shoes, too, black as night, strange looking hooves one might use on the moon.

"These will keep you warm and protect you from parasites or biting insects. Warm, cold, doesn't matter…military grade," he said, his face beaming with pride. "One size, they stretch and shrink from your body heat. They're not much to look at," he shrugged. "But you'll be glad you wore them." I nodded along like an idiot.

"Even snakes can't bite through."

"Snakes?"

"Where you heading?" he asked, the small talk looming larger. Perhaps in Neville's line of business, this innocuous bedside manner was a stock of the trade, something to make those who were guiltily uncomfortable, more comfortable.

"Somewhere west. Did you say snakes?"

"The device knows you're going?" he asked with raised eyebrows and flared nostrils.

"Not sure."

"Unusual," Neville said as I fumbled through the equipment on the counter. His smile made up for his abnormal look. Despite his misfortune, he appeared content, even happy.

"Enjoy your day. You never know when it's your last one," he continued, the full lips carrying that same damp smile. Then he used a strange term, an Echo term evidently, that Harriet would soon use—something about a "Last hurrah."

"Thank you," I said after a pause to find something equally philosophical to say. I found nothing. What a strange little man this Neville.

I forgot to mention, Neville's head was bare as a dinner plate and nearly as smooth and shiny. It was strange to see this deserted pate (I could see my own reflection in the oily sheen clear as day), as baldness had gone out of style along with crooked teeth, dry skin and the most egregious of disease. Before our transaction was complete, he covered his head with a brown, raked fedora, one like the old-time gangsters used to wear. I suppose it was a purposeful endeavor on his part, part of the intimidation and price negotiation, or something encouraged by central casting.

I've heard of his type, Neville, switched out when the first one failed, "the old switch-a-roo" as Harriet would say. Here was one in front of me, the original likely dead and gone and his Echo raised up in his stead. I dare say I could tell the difference, but I couldn't. He was useful, you see, so there were exceptions to the ways of the device. There always are. Consistency is a virtuous ideal embraced by the device. Everything else is a mystery.

Neville, and I assume others like him, is allowed to operate his malevolent business out of a tenuous kindness.

And, like a drain plug on a burgeoning sink, even the slightest nudge could trigger a deluge, taking the entire operation down. The people (or whomever or whatever) who operate the device could have him snuffed out if they so wished, disappeared him in an instant, but he's allowed to distribute his black-market wares and back-alley potions as a sort of morbid cultural exchange. I've found people are often happiest when they believe they're getting away with something, however small, pushing the boundaries taut, but without snapping the rope. Harriet said the equipment we acquired "fell off the back of a truck." Neville provided just such a service. And, after all, we all need to make a living.

When our initial transaction was complete, I (finally) had a look around the room. It wasn't a glance but a serious and necessary viewing. In truth, I was a bit nerved up to be in such a place, as I'd heard stories of people never returning from just such errands as mine. Neville had noted the look, my look, a thousand times, ten times over a measure of a day.

"Not to worry," he said with the satisfied smile of a man at the top of his game before beginning his well-honed speech.

"All radio frequencies are jammed." [No one can listen to us.]

"The walls, ceiling and floors are magnetized." [We cannot be mapped.]

"The ventilation is filtered and cooled." [We cannot be sniffed out or thermally imaged and our DNA is being scrubbed.]

"Technically, I'm dead." [I was never here, therefore, neither were you.]

He raised his eyebrows though I was sure he didn't anticipate any further questions, and I half expected him to take a deep and purposeful bow, fedora held tight against his heart.

"And the red triangle?" I asked, now greedy with new found confidence. I'd become emboldened by his cheeky and convincing leveling of the facts. "Can you get some of that?"

He eyed me up and down like he was wondering who I might be, which branch of the intelligence service issued my paycheck. Had he somehow underestimated my meek and dour exterior? He hadn't.

"A connoisseur of the ales of Old England, are we?" he asked, his head tilted forward, the thin brim of his hat hiding his eyes. Until now, I was unsure whether the hat was meant to further his manufactured persona or to prevent the lights from scorching his naked scalp. "I thought you were just a run of the mill Mid-Lev."

He was counting in his head, gears turning, engaging the wheels of commerce. "Tuesday," he said. I nodded.

Before he let me leave, he hoisted the brim of his hat with the thumb of his right hand, exposing his brown eyes and thick, meandering brow. "Can you put in a good word for me with your sister-law?" he asked. His demeanor had changed in an instant and he appeared childlike, a bashful adolescent seeking a date to the prom.

"Anna?" I asked.

"Yes, yes, the lovely Anna," he said with a slippery laugh. "She's a good customer and generally fond of you."

Anna, of course, had directed me to Neville and his underground flea circus, but I hadn't considered the fact she herself may be in need of the goods and services he may or may not provide.

"By the way," he said as I waited for the elevator to whisk me back to the surface, to freedom. "If you ever need anything, things that may be *difficult* to acquire, you know who to ask."

"Do you mean things like NECCO wafers?" I immediately felt silly for asking and slumped my shoulders forward, careful to not look him in the eye.

"Yeah, things like that," he said, the damp grin on his face expanding. Whatever goodwill I'd managed to create was unceremoniously dumped on the floor and pulled down an unseen drain.

"Thank you," I said again over the gurgling of the drain.

I wasn't sure exactly what to make of Neville. Along with his unorthodox manner, he carried the unearned confidence of one who falsely believes they're in charge of something relevant. Though he'd been subdued in my presence, he had a reputation for making outlandish claims, boasting of clients both well-heeled and well-connected, and nurtured a mysterious, intimidating atmosphere an intelligence officer would admire. I have to admit, though, he was able to secure the gear we requested with little notice (not to mention the ale). Perhaps there was some substance to his boasts. After all, Anna saw something in him.

The lighting in the elevator was mottled and stretched—much different than the intense, focused light of the office. I asked to be brought to the surface to which there was no response. Had I already forgotten my last elevator ride not a half hour prior? It was an old, cranky thing with metal push buttons laid out in three or four rows and columns. One of the buttons had a star on it—I figured this was the one to press. In another life, was this elevator equipped to raise you into the sky, to the stars or was being raised from the basement a sign that things were looking up? The elevator door slid closed with a surprisingly smooth hiss and thump. Once the seal of the door was tight, the air around me grew fresh, more familiar, like coming home. For the first time in my life, I felt a little dirty, a low in the hips prodigal. Deep below the membrane, my skin began to itch. It was exhilarating! And when the door slid open to reveal the surface light it was like I'd stolen an oven warm loaf of bread at the open market, shoved it beneath my jacket and melted into the unsuspecting crowd.

Lark
(The Hike)

The black-market gear was made of tough but comfortable fabric that stretched in every direction and the shoes had ceramic nails protruding from the bottom. What a sight we were that day! The jacket and pants, sewn together to make a suit for frontier travel, were a florescent "rescue green." Since the fabrics reduced our heat signature to almost nil, the rescue green color was our only hope of detection should we find ourselves in need of detecting. Especially, as Neville noted with a wink, if we fell victim to snake bites.

The transport slowed to a hover near a weathered metal trailhead marker bolted to a large, gray rock. We'd left the city before sunrise and slept during the hour-long transit. The frontier revealed its secrets at first light. It was greener than I'd expected: sturdy, thick-trunked trees, tall and full-leafed, rolling hills and fields heavy with grass and thorn bushes. It was spectacular! Even wildlife had returned in surprising numbers to what was once barren and strip-mined.

I'd never heard so many songbirds in full voice. For a few moments, I was unable to move, captivated by their singing, mesmerized by their quick, fluttering movements like a feline prowling across a bay window. I'd seen and heard birds before, of course, but never in such numbers or in such obvious health. Contrary to what I'd read, the earth, after suffering grave wounds, was healing. For the first time in my life there were no people, and buildings didn't stretch upward toward the sky until they blotted out both the sun and the ancient light. With great risk of ignorance and the repeating of past sins, the resources before me appeared plentiful and infinite.

Before I'd time to take it all in, Harriet hit the trail at great speed, her shoes clawing the dirt path and her body hurling forward like gravity no longer applied. When I finally caught up to her (she was patiently waiting for me), I reached out to give her a hug, but she bounded away like a fawn escaping a cougar. She was energized by the freedom of open space, renewed, invigorated. I, meanwhile, failed to keep pace and if not for her backtracking may have fallen far enough behind to be thankful for the rescue green.

When we reached the peak, I was tired and useless, worn thin. Harriet, however, had yet to hit her stride and seemed disappointed the five miles had so easily been scaled. There was a clearing at the top of the trail that overlooked a valley and another rise of mountains in the distance. It served as both a resting spot and objective. I was happy (and somewhat surprised) to have reached it.

"We did this every day," she said prowling the length of

the clearing to burn excess energy. "Patrols and training."

"Some of us don't get out much," I said, bent at the waist in a fruitless attempt to gain my breath, my heart beating in rapid thumps. Despite the membrane, I was covered in perspiration.

"That's obvious," she said and laughed at my pathetic state, my exhaustion, my perfect reflection of a modern man.

There was something in my shoe, a stone digging and rubbing raw the thin skin on the arch of my foot. I would have stopped to remove it during the climb, but I feared being left further behind, abandoned to the wolves (and snakes). I flopped to the ground in a heap before digging out the offending chunk of earth. I pinched it between my fingers and studied it, grey and white, a small stone, but a provider of infinite pain. Such stones were another of nature's hazards we'd swept clean from the city. We'd removed the impediments from daily life and made it one less unpleasantness we'd need to avoid in our lives of relative ease. In society, there were no longer stones in anyone's shoes.

"You wouldn't last the night," she noted. She crossed her arms tightly across her chest and looked at me down the length of her nose. I don't believe she'd intended it as a jest.

"No," I agreed. Not even a night. "People live here though, mountain folk." I shrugged in case I was wrong or foolish enough to believe the children's stories and the myths. "At least that's the legend."

"There are people here," she said and spun around slowly to look in all directions. "But you'll never see them. They're people who don't want to be seen."

I was still on the ground, fumbling, one shoe off, staring off into the infinite green of the valley that had unfolded before us as we climbed.

"Why did you take me here?" she asked.

"Talis used to tell me about trips with her father into these mountains," I said. "She loves it here. She asked me many times if we could go together, I guess so she could show me, but I never agreed. I never wanted to go."

"Why now?" She asked.

"I have a second chance. I want to see what I missed. I want to be happy and I think, maybe I am now." My admission felt heavy and too soon, but I couldn't take it back. I squinted to see her standing above me, the sun casting her in a glowing silhouette.

"Is that the goal in life, in your society, happiness?"

Did she scoff or did she really want to know?

"It took a long time for me to realize it, and I think it is, yes. This is your society now, too." I'd finally stopped sweating. Neville and his damn suits.

Harriet didn't respond. Her mauve eyes stared over the valley, her mouth rigid and preoccupied. Her hands were firmly on her hips and the early afternoon sun reddened her cheeks and neck. She couldn't stop staring at the vastness of it. I'm sure she heard me.

"Tell me what it is you like about me," she said.

"I like your laugh, and the way you make me laugh with your strange phrases and sayings. I like your scent. I like the way you taste. I like the curves of your body," I said. "You're not like everyone else."

"I'm imperfect?"

"Yes, you are. But that's what makes you special."

She was still staring over the valley, toward the expanse of nature with soft white clouds hovering toward the horizon. There was a slight breeze that carried the scent of pine trees and far away storm clouds. All was quiet.

"Most of all," I said. "I like how I feel when we're together."

"Do I make you happy?" she asked.

"Yes."

"Do I make you feel free?"

"Yes."

"Is this what you want?"

"Yes." I never thought I'd admit it.

"Your last hurrah."

(Ten soldiers)

Ten soldiers stood in silence at the bottom of trench Five-Thirty, their arms tight against their sides and their bodies aligned in a rigid line. The light of the first quarter moon reflected in the runoff of a scheduled rain as it streamed down the trench walls and filled the bottom with ankle deep mud. Walter removed a narrow notebook from his waterproof pack. He looked each soldier in the eye, walking down the line, pausing briefly at each soldier, eye to eye, nose to nose.

The notebook, handed to him by the Sargent-Major, carried specific protocol: to be opened in trench Five-Thirty in the presence of these ten soldiers, on this specific date and at this specific time. It was a black lab notebook with a glued spine and narrow blue lines on white pages and a small white square on the cover with lines for a title. In the title box was written the trench number, Walter's name as well as Harriet's and the names of the eight other soldiers who stood in the mud at the bottom of this trench on this date, at this time. The notebook was tightly wrapped in a clear, waterproof (and, presumably, mud-proof) membrane.

Before removing the membrane, Walter took attendance. Each solider responded to their name with a low refrain of "here," barely audible above the sounds of flowing rainwater and distant wind in the trees. When all ten soldiers were confirmed present, Walter removed the curved knife from its sheath and slid it between the membrane and the notebook, carefully slicing it open.

Within the pages of the notebook were handwritten orders, an overview of the assignment followed by pages with individualized instructions and details for each soldier. There were no dates or times assigned to the instructions, save one: the date and time the first orders would commence. In addition to orders similar in scope to the other nine soldiers, an ancillary assignment for Captain Walter was written in red ink. He was tasked with the unthinkable.

—

The ten soldiers spent eight weeks isolated in trench Five-Thirty. They ate together. They stood guard together. They endured artillery and burning red gel and ankle-deep mud that grew a little deeper each day. During that time, the contents of the notebook were read and re-read, digested and committed to memory. Soldiers were expected to know their role, to embrace it and be able to repeat it verbatim to Captain Walter.

Once a week, Captain Walter emerged from the mud, climbed the ladder up the trench wall and set off to resupply and provide progress reports to the Sargent-Major.

Questions from each soldier concerning their assignments were handwritten by Captain Walter into the margins of the notebook, while answers from the Sargent-Major were written below each question by the same hand. Security protocol required the Captain and Sargent-Major to meet at a different location each week and the specific location coordinates of the meetings were kept secret until the last possible moment. They always met outdoors with the precise location known only to the Sargent-Major and his courier who escorted the Captain to the meeting location.

The nameless courier was a tall, slender man with gray eyes, reddish-brown skin and a perpetually clean shave. He was known for his immaculate cleanliness: his teeth were scrubbed three times a day, his ears purged of wax on a weekly basis, and the crescent of grime lodged beneath his fingernails—well, there wasn't any. In short, the crispness of his uniform and shine of his boots screamed that he wasn't trench material and he was glad for it.

When the courier arrived at trench Five-Thirty, he presented the Captain handwritten coordinates sealed in a white envelope, a redundancy should the courier fall or suffer capture before delivering the Captain. The date and time of the next meeting, but not the location, was agreed upon at the end of each meeting. If it became necessary to meet before the next scheduled meeting, the courier would arrive to fetch the Captain or set a new meeting time. If the Captain was to request a meeting, he sent one of his soldiers to place a green ribbon on an old-growth oak at an intersection of two roads. This ribbon would alert the courier who would arrive the same day to make the arrangements.

"I assume you have some questions yourself," the Sargent-Major said to Walter one afternoon at a scheduled meeting during an unscheduled rain. "You have a very important job."

"No, sir," Walter replied, his hair was tight to his head, recently cut, rainwater rolled down his forehead and into his eyes causing him to blink excessively. "I have no questions."

"This order comes from high up, from someone at the device."

"Yes, sir."

"Do you understand what's expected of you?"

"Yes, sir."

"Do you understand why it needs to be done?"

"It's not my place to understand why," Walter replied.

"Very good, Captain."

"Actually, I do have one question, Sargent-Major."

"Yes, Captain."

"When?"

"I don't have that answer, Captain. I will summon you when the time arrives. Be ready. Stay focused."

The pace of rain quickened as Walter awaited his dismissal. It was a cold, driving rain that formed deep puddles and splashed mud onto his black boots. There's always mud yet I'm still distraught when my boots are dirty, Walter thought to himself. Other than the sound of the rain, the forest was quiet and aloof, like it inhaled a secret and was unwilling to exhale.

In the eyes of Echoes, there are two types of war: conventional and personal. A conventional war consists of heavy equipment, artillery, aircraft, warships, large armies and large-scale conflict. Conventional war intends to alter geography and secure resources, to smote an enemy and impose your will while accomplishing objectives on grand scales. Conventional war envelopes all in its path regardless of conscious participation.

Personal war is a war of assassination and sabotage, small-scale conflicts used to achieve limited, high-value objectives. This war of secret knocks and deciphered code aims to minimize collateral damage and maximize effort and value. Out of necessity, the Echoes are adept at both.

Trench Five-Thirty was five hundred yards long, and Walter walked its length to find an area free of eyes and ears, an area of seclusion in which to prepare. "Be ready. Stay focused." Those were the words of the Sargent-Major that indicated the task was imminent and he must begin the process of separating his thoughts, his emotions, his humanity from his given profession. No other soldiers approached him. His stomach was turned upside down. He needed it right side up. This malevolent business left little room for guilt and even less for emotion.

Several days earlier, he'd set a small stool at the bottom of the trench, and now it was time to sit. His mind drifted far away as he whittled away extraneous thoughts, attempting to focus on one specific objective. He retrieved a spool of wire from one of the front pockets of his pack and strung a length of the micro-thin metal between his index fingers, and using his thumbs to guide the wire, cleared the narrow spaces between his teeth, one by one. If his gums bled from the wire, he needed to be more precise in his movements, more disciplined in his approach. No amount of scar tissue or calloused gums could resist the wire's onslaught. Unsteady hands were the enemy. Blood, sweet and metallic, filled his mouth. He spat the red failure on the ground, forming small, thick puddles at his feet. He would need to concentrate. He would need to be better. His time was growing near.

He awoke from his trance to the sound of footsteps and the slosh of mud, the approach of a determined, reckless gait. He wouldn't last an afternoon, Walter thought to himself and smiled. The courier stood in front of Walter and stared down disappointedly at his own muddied boots. He'd arrived to congratulate him. Walter's prize: a one-day leave.

The next morning a transport whisked him to a nearby military installation. In accordance with established policy, he was showered and scanned for viruses and radiation, his bowels were scanned for parasites and heavy metals. The warm shower water ran black into the drain as weeks of mud were cleansed from his skin. He shaved and brushed his teeth. He trimmed his fingernails and toenails and dug the grime from underneath both with the sharp, pointed fork of the curved knife. He was provided access to deodorant, cologne and fresh clothes. A haircut was unnecessary as each trench team was provided a kit and a comb would have garnered little friction on his recently shorn skull.

Military leaves were issued by the device like arranged marriages, and assuming compatibility (and continued health), were long-term obligations. In Walter's case, he'd been granted leave with the same woman for almost five years. They'd grown fond of each other to the point where they looked forward to their next leave for more than physical contact—they enjoyed each other's company. While leaves were not scheduled (at least not by the soldiers), Walter concluded he could expect one to be granted one every fifty to seventy days. He assumed this early leave, after only forty days, was a reward for the tasks he'd yet to accomplish.

She was from trench Eighty-Seven, olive skinned and blue eyed and walked with the confidence he only dreamed he could possess. She also wore the black sheath and curved knife. They formed an instant bond—two peas in a pod. If this were ancient times filled with ancient optimism, one might remark they'd found their soul mate. Sometimes the device and human nature worked together seamlessly. Often, they did not.

After Walter met her for the first time, their first leave, he thanked the Sargent-Major for his good taste and for considering him for this match. It was an unnecessary and misguided gesture as the Sargent-Major had little stomach for matchmaking and little power to influence these decisions.

"No, no," he said. "I had nothing to do with it. Simply some good luck on your part."

But, in truth, he had everything to do with it. The almost

five-year relationship of convenience was never meant as a utilitarian gesture with little more significance than a holiday away from the office. Good luck didn't exist. This was an arrangement not created out of convenience, but out of necessity. The direction was from the top: introduce them as partners on leave, nurture their bond, await further instructions. Nearly five years later, the latest instructions were drawn down the chain of command—handwritten orders that eventually landed in a black cover lab notebook at the bottom of trench Five-Thirty. Utilizing the outlined methodology five years in the making, the device predicted a ninety-seven percent chance of success.

Walter, carrying an army green duffle, was whisked by transport to an old hunting lodge built into the side of a mountain. It was a grand building constructed of wood and nails with peaked turrets and stately gables and a porch that wrapped around nearly three-quarters the building. Although they'd been sent to this location on many leaves, it was the first time they were granted a room on the third floor, a large, formal suite with a living room fireplace and large, tiled bathroom with mirrors that filled nearly every wall. He arrived first and set a wood fire, warming the rooms and filling the suite with a subtle scent of burning hardwood. He found a white, silk robe folded in a closet, and he laid it full-length on the bed to entice her to wear it.

Her favorite flower was primrose, and he requested blue, pink, white and yellow primrose placed in vases of various sizes and shapes be staged around the suite. He saved her favorite primrose, Blue Zebra, for the bedroom itself. She'd told him Blue Zebra made her happiest and, when she saw them, she wrapped her arms around him and thanked him for his thoughtfulness. Though her eyes were closed tightly, he imagined their deep blue, sparkling with an ability to see through him, to see past any ruse. Maybe once, this once, she wouldn't.

In the evening, he ran a hot bath. Intended as the center-piece of the room, the bathtub was a clawfoot iron beast set in a commanding position near the middle of the bathroom. On one end were silver faucets and levers and the other was an elongated curve and decline allowing the bather to lean back into a comfortable lounging position. The ancient water levers took great strength to turn and control, and the temperature and flow of water were fickle, uncooperative. Eventually, he was able to work the water temperature to a satisfactory hot. He added oils and soaps to the simmering cauldron, bits of this and that, things he'd found in one of the cabinets, and a small vile of lavender he'd stashed from her last visit. From the bed and wearing the white robe, she heard water filling the vessel and caught the scent of laven-der. He remembered her favorite scent.

After a few minutes spent considering her ideal entrance, she made her way into the bathroom in a bobbing, slow trot, the pads of her bare feet slapping frivolously against the cold tile. She looked over the scene, taking in the moment, hands at her waist and neck craned over the tub like a pageant judge while Walter periodically tested the water temperature with a gentle splash of his hand. When the water reached halfway to the top, she untied the robe and shimmied her shoulders, left then right, left then right, rolling the ball of her shoulders to loosen the robe. The robe slid to the floor in a slow, deliberate slither down the length of her body. She stood nude in front of the tub, teasing, staring at his reflection in the mirror. He gestured his arm, hand and fingers extended toward the tub and said, "For you."

"Will you join me?" she asked.

"I may, but not yet," he said before squeezing the faucet closed with a heavy turn of his wrist.

"I'll be lonely. Let me know if I can change your mind."

"You can relax now," he said. "Dream of whatever you wish. Dream of far-away places and adventures. Release any thoughts that don't make you happy."

"This is just the treat I needed," she said. "I feel like a gilded lady."

He held one of her hands, steadying her as she stepped over the high sides of the clawfoot, one leg, then the other, like it was her first time entering a bath. Indeed, it was.

Barbara spent a half hour relaxing in the hot water, eyes closed, leaning back into the curve of the tub while the scent of lavender floated in the air. At the sound of his footsteps, she opened her eyes and watched in the mirror across the room as he approached from behind. She did little to defend herself, either accepting of whatever fate had mustered, or remaining too trusting of Walter, too trusting of her soulmate. He knelt at her end of the tub and, in one smooth motion, flipped the wire over her head and across her throat, cross-crossed his hands behind her before he drew the wire snug against the delicate skin of her neck.

Small beads of blood formed where the wire met her throat, the metal cold against her skin while blood warmed her neck. She understood it was an indefensible position, her throat bared to a razor wire, a trained, willing killer wielding it. All was lost. This was the end. Only a stoic, soldierly acceptance remained. She'd been trained not to question, only to obey orders and she knew he, too, was following orders. She wouldn't live long enough to learn the reason and, besides, she was too proud to ask.

Walter wrapped the wire around his hands, pulling it taut around her neck. The wire gave slack as it sliced her skin, severing her windpipe clean when he applied the perfected strength of an assassin. She attempted a last, hopeless breath and thrust her arms into the air before her body fell limp, the sparkle abandoning her blue eyes. Blood escaped from her neck, pouring over her breasts before staining the water a cloudy, dark crimson.

When it was done, he walked to the other side of the tub and placed his hand into the still hot water. He pulled the drain plug, drawing the crimson water downward in a devil's whirlpool. He collapsed on the floor beside the tub, one hand holding onto the rim, the other covering his eyes, hiding behind either embarrassment or regret. He sat motionless, unable or unwilling to continue—he was unsure which. As the water drained from the tub, now flowed the assassin's guilt, a wrenching only present when the assassin is intimately familiar with its quarry. He breathed in deep, expanding his chest to burst, and released the air in a slow, steady stream. The next step was the most difficult…the most personal.

Iris scans were the standard method of identification and of particular interest for the military. In the early days, when the technology was less evolved, it was standard security procedure to remove the eyes of soldiers who fell in the field and return them for storage or disposal. It was a deeply personal act that few soldiers could fully reconcile. In modern times, it was no longer a security necessity, but had morphed into an unofficial tradition, the act of preserving the eyes so, even in death, they may continue to watch over their comrades, continue to open doors to the future. It was considered an act of honor, but it was only practiced by one segment of the military.

Walter removed the curved blade from the black sheath stored on the bed along with Barbara's folded uniform—the sheath Barbara had carried for decades.

His final words to her as he drew her own knife in his steady hands: "I'm sorry, Barbara. You trusted me. I couldn't know you shouldn't."

Holding Barbara's blade, he used the forked tongue to dig behind her eye socket and pry out the formerly sparkling blues, then cut the connecting tissue to release each one. He removed the small cylinder from the sheath, opened the lid and slid each eyeball into the liquid inside and sealed it.

He then used the curved blade to cut two short pieces of blood-soaked wire and pulled out a fine metal needle that was embedded into the sheath. The wire was threaded through the needle and he took one last, deep inhale through his nose then sewed both of her eyelids closed with small, delicate loops. The wire was pulled through the fine skin with the skill of a surgeon. Small droplets of blood formed on Barbara's lids with each stroke of the needle, each loop of wire.

"It's done, Sargent-Major," he said, but there was no response.

"It's done," he repeated. There was no response.

"This is Walter for Sargent-Major."

The room was quiet save the continuing sound of blood dripping, gurgling into the mouth of the tub drain. Walter began to search for signs of its presence, pacing the suite and pacing it again. There could be a malfunction, but he'd never encountered operational distress. After a thorough search, he found no traces. It was the first structure he'd entered that was not monitored by the device.

He retrieved a small, black, quick-response bag from the duffle he'd placed in the one corner of the bedroom. The black bag was constructed of a liquid proof membrane that stretched many times its size and was chiefly used to carry deceased soldiers. After removing Barbara from the tub, he gently placing her into the membrane before sealing it.

His transport wasn't scheduled to arrive until morning and without the device, there was no way to summon it earlier. He tended the small wood fire in the living room fireplace and spent the evening seated in front of it attempting to empty his mind of all thoughts and to clear his conscience.

When he returned to the trench, additional instructions awaited in the pages of the black notebook.

Talis
(Something Arrives)

My hands were heavy and the skin wrinkled and angry as if it were preparing to flay itself away from my bones and flee. Large, rhythmic tremors shook my entire body and my teeth chattered. My lips were salty from tears that momentarily rested on the small upward curve of skin below my nose before cresting into my mouth as each new tremor erupted. I was seated on the bathroom floor unable, and unwilling, to move. There were smears of crimson on the white floor tile, each a guilty crescent left behind as I attempted to escape across the room by crawling backward on my palms, using my arms to propel my body, to move away from my leaking self. I came to rest against the wall, unable to crawl further, my legs splayed out in front of me while the fog of hot water filled the room with dreamy clouds. All was dissembled now, my body altered and transformed, then matured as I slid…and leaked. Had it worked itself back together into something more desirable, more functional? Had I arrived in heaven or had I simply arrived?

Where else could I be? What else could it be?

A knock on the door.

"Don't come in!" I screamed.

"Are you alright?"

"Don't come in!" I repeated louder.

There was a calm in his voice that didn't match his words, "You sound like you're in distress."

"Ummm…no. Yes. I don't know."

"Should the device summon help?" he asked.

"Holy Fuck! NO!"

Walter was speaking to the device on the other side of the door, his voice remained measured, his words calmly paced. "No that won't be necessary, there's no need."

The response from the device was muffled, vague and far away, lost in the fluffy steam and maniacal red smears. I couldn't hear it clearly.

"There's some blood, yes, but from her nose, probably due to the dry air. That must be what you detect," Walter answered. I envisioned him shrugging politely and summoning a fake laugh. "Yes, good idea. I'll adjust the humidity now."

I couldn't speak. Bile rose high into my throat and mouth and I became hot, disoriented. I gagged then wretched, leaving a small pool of brownish liquid on the tile beside me. Today, I was an artist painting a floor of many colors.

"How did you know about the blood?" I asked through the door.

The room was silent save the continuing splash of water onto the shower walls and the whistle of air moving heavily through my nostrils, whining like a boiling kettle on a lonely Sunday afternoon.

"Isn't this what you wanted?" Walter responded. He was steady when you found yourself in a pinch, so sure of himself. The soldier's training, no doubt. Someone I wanted on my team, a team in desperate need of a new member.

"Yes… I don't know," I responded. "I'm dying. I think there's a hemorrhage." It was the only logical explanation and I was glad Walter was there, someone to help with the cleaning and identifying the body and all that rest.

There was laughing from the other side of the door. It was a deep laugh of satisfaction. "You're not dying, " he said. "You're living."

I asked again, "How did you know I was bleeding?"

"I noticed it before, earlier," he said. "I'm sorry I didn't tell you. I thought you'd know what it was when you saw it."

"How could I possibly know?" I shouted.

"You couldn't, of course," he said in a softer voice. "May I come in?"

"No!" I shouted. "I made a mess in here—don't come in! There's a...it's…no, don't come in."

I rose to my feet by leaning back against the wall and using my hands to climb. Once I was standing, I leaned into the wall and shuffled my feet along the tile until I reached the still steaming shower. Hot water streamed over my body and rolled downward toward the tile floor, steam filled my lungs and made me cough. A puddle of pink water swirled on the bottom of the shower creating a rose-colored tint around the white skin of my feet before being pulled down the drain with an apathetic gulp.

"This is not supposed to happen, not to me," I said out loud, then repeated it to myself in a shaky voice that echoed off the walls of the shower and bathroom. I could still taste salty tears though they were diluted, rinsed away as quickly as they fell onto my lips. For how long could one cry? Once I asked that question, I felt a calm beginning to take hold, like a shadow from a passing cloud had caught up to me after a days long chase, providing a respite from the heat of the mid-day sun.

"Yes, it is," he said, his words confident, almost scholarly in tone. "It is supposed to happen to you. There's no one more deserving." I could feel his smirk, that wonderful smile, pushing forward through the door, through the mist. Then he was gone.

What did Walter know? What could Walter know?

While staring into the translucent mirror across the room I saw my body, contorted and thin, ghost white in the mist, staring back at me, and I asked myself: What do I do now?

I pulled in deep, wet breaths and released them slowly, attempting to moderate my racing heart rate. I was naked and alone. I'd been naked before, of course, since my birth, but for the first time in my life I felt nude, a beauty cast in oil on canvas, a complete and romanticized version of myself. All I could do was stare at this stranger and wonder who she was meant to become.

There's always a sense of nakedness, especially in situations that make us uncomfortable or embarrassed. But none compared to this, nothing was as thoroughly freeing and potent as my arrival, despite the awkward and mysterious journey I'd taken. The journey, after all, must be enjoyed, savored, and tasted, if the ends have any chance of success.

Lark
(End)

Harriet's on her way back here, to her apartment in Holtsford Park. She's always running late and is often forgetful. Part of her charm, I guess. A couple weeks ago she asked the device to allow my iris scan—the equivalent of that ancient gesture of giving your significant other a key. Today I let myself in. As Harriet said, I guess that makes us "an item."

Last we spoke, her tone was peculiar and she was out of breath, rushed, exasperated, like she was running late for an appointment with no obvious place to be. Over the past month, she's grown distant, loving, yes, but her mind is preoccupied with weighty thoughts, her nights spent on the fringes of sleep. When I awaken in the dead of night (which happens often), she's usually awake, staring up at the ceiling, likely counting each imperfection in the paint and each imperfection in her life and each one of my imperfections. Perhaps, like the rest of us, she's struggling to understand her place in the world.

I'm not the most important thing in her life, though I want to be. I can be smothering—another one of my own myriad charms. But things have changed and her beautiful mauve eyes no longer see me clearly. Her eyes no longer see a prince dressed in finery, perched upon a royal steed, my enemies vanquished by blade or spear, my peasant's bellies full and safe for another night. Instead, they look down toward my feet or past me, like they've grown bored of my presence or gone stale and begun to rot while stored in the cellar. Not that I could blame her. I've become a thing to pity, a pig to be ignored, unnamed and soft, fattened up for the approaching holiday.

When I mentioned it was our anniversary of sorts, six months of unrepentant bliss, she only found the energy for a sad little smile, a tepid acknowledgement of the half-year tryst. Despite my theory that apathy carried a degree of attraction, it was not panning out. I hadn't expected a dance on the tabletop or tribal hoots of celebration, but I also didn't expect my Harriet to turn dour—for my mauve rose to wither and waste away. All the women in my life push me away. No, they push away from me. I possess just enough charm to remain expendable. Call it a gift. I was never comfortable with change.

She's also been dropping little hints, words of warning, like a canine baring its teeth after you've finally mustered the courage to pat its damp nose. I'm not foolish, I'm not, as Harriet would say, "out to lunch." At least not overly "out to lunch." Or perhaps I'm so out to lunch, I've already taken a lemming-like plunge off the cliff. Pride's sibling is closer than I thought.

The green light on the device is glowing, pulsating like a balloon threatening to burst—there's a message from Talis that I'm choosing to ignore. I don't know how long it's been waiting for me and I haven't found the heart or energy to listen to it. Something inside me says it's another self-righteous lecture, and I'm not in the mood to withstand the onslaught. She has such vitriol—not necessarily with me, but because of me. I've generously contributed to that fund for many years, building it up to bloat and fattened it to where she is now. I've found so many uses for pig metaphors. I have so many things to tell her—obviously she has something to say also.

I want to tell her one day: I let go, but only because you let go already a long time ago. I understand why you did. I'm not saying I forgive you and I'm not expecting you to forgive me. It's too late for that. It's too late for us. There's too little time and too much harm done. We now follow whatever path remains in front of us. The road no longer forks but runs straight ahead, full forward. We need to start living again before it's too late. Both of us. Most of all, I want her to know I still love her. I don't know if that will bring her any comfort, but it does for me. The stench of failure is difficult to mitigate despite an honest lifetime of soap and chamois.

Harriet asked me something peculiar the other day. Maybe the question wasn't so odd, maybe I was odd in my reception of it, in the way I internalized it, the thoughts it managed to stir. The question flowed naturally from her and, despite the weight, it didn't alter her demeanor. Perhaps she'd been asked the very same question a hundred times, but to me, it was unfamiliar. It was more jargon of the Echoes and their foreign, dated dialect and their foreign, dated way of thinking. But it's a thinking that will outlast us all.

We were seated at our favorite spot, a sidewalk table outside the Café Drame, our heavy metal chairs somehow unsteady and uncomfortable despite a thousand years of chair design and little evolution of the human spine. The wind was scheduled to dilute at sundown and the temperature was moderated to 21 degrees Celsius. My favorite place had, with time and music and glasses of warm absinthe, become her favorite place as well. She loved to sit outside on Thursday evenings when the café was alive with music that she referred to with the strange moniker, "American Standards." The songs, to my ears, were an emptied jar, crooning tomes of lost loves and a questionable affinity for gambling and specific old towns. She immersed herself in these songs and knew them rote, her beautiful eyes pulled closed and her lips singing along like she grew up with them emanating from her mother's device on Sunday afternoons. But I knew that wasn't possible.

Her question was serious, but delivered in a playful tone: "What do you want to be when you grow up?"

There must be endless answers to this simple question disguised as a philosophical paradox. I'm still stunned. Or perhaps taken aback is more accurate. Not because of the question (though it was unusual) but because of my answer or the weakness of my answer. The lack of an answer. After searching and thinking and considering, wracking my brain for an honest riposte (there must be one), all I could conjure was: "Not this."

No, "not this," is a boy's answer (not a man's), a boy with bountiful time to spare, with optimism to spare, enough time to adjust the sail and harness the change in the wind, enough time to improvise, to learn, before ripening and growing old. The whole affair made me uncomfortable. Why would I ponder this when life was so easily changed, without consent, mashed into a lumpy paste by a string of code? Stumped, I did what anyone in my position would, I closed my eyes and tugged on the parachute's ripcord. I turned it on its heels and asked the same question of her.

"I have grown up," she said and shrugged her shoulders. A thin, but satisfied smile leaked from her mouth. "I am who I want to be."

"And who is that?"

"You're not blind, Lark, don't act blinded!" She barked. "You don't live under a rock!"

There, now her eyes were fixed upon me! This version of her was as slippery as a snake, her eyes devoid of life, empty, but even serpents are known to be right on occasion and their path, though not always prudent, is always clear.

There are some truths to a civilized society in decline, but they are presented as questions rather than answers or paradoxes to ponder: What do you do when there's too much bacteria in the water? What do you do when the alleys are filled with rats? What do you do when there are too many mouths to feed? What do you do when you've become the pest? What do you do when you grow up?

I can't shake the notion and fact that there are too many of us, and I know it doesn't end well. There's nothing to do but wait. The hammer will fall. It always does. Like many of our most personal decisions, it's all been decided for us. The pressure is off. I've finally accepted we're the end of our line. Hiding, of course, is fruitless and pointless, it's not a game of hide-and-go-seek with its so-called winners, and losers. If there are winners, we're not to know. Like many truths in life, many histories, only the winners will be privy.

There's a message from Harriet also, a strange, desperate message even for her.

"Lark, understand that I love you. In this life there are no heroes or villains, there are no punishments or rewards, it just is. We make the decisions. It's 5:30."

Oh, it's you. You're finally here. Is there something I'm supposed to have for you? Forgive me, but I'm not familiar with the procedure.

Was I supposed to prepare some kind of speech? I was never one for speeches. Or do you have something to say to me? Tell me how this is supposed to go. There was a reason, I knew there was a reason I just didn't know what. It couldn't have been simply a coincidence and it certainly wasn't out of kindness. There's always a plan even if we're unaware. There's always a plan. I'm glad you agree.

Time? No, it's past 5:30. I see, that's not the point, is it?

You just let yourself in! I'm not surprised by bad behavior, then again, I'm not sure what behavior to expect.

Am I supposed to welcome you? There's no need to be grumpy. Look at the predicament I'm in yet I'm not grumpy. Maybe that does make me better than you, yes.

How did you get in anyway? Oh, I see. That makes sense. They are the same. Very clever. I knew something was off. Our eyes are so close they can fool the scanner? So much for security.

And you've dragged mud into the house! Where are your manners? Could you at least have done something about those boots? They're filthy! So much mud! No, no, it's too late now.

You are a fine-looking specimen, though that shouldn't surprise anyone.

Why are you pointing? Do you want me to sit? More than happy to—tell me and tell me the truth—why are you here? Yes, I know why, but I'd like to hear it from you. I need you to say it.

Yes, yes, I'll sit, there's no reason to give me that look and certainly not an attitude. Yes, we should've known, I should've known. It made too much sense but please don't patronize me now. It's too late for it and it's bad manners.

What? Of course, I'm wearing clean underwear! No, my mother didn't tell me that. Is that something she should have told me? If she did, I missed that lecture. It's customary?

Evidently you can learn something new each day.

Do these need to be so tight? They hurt my wrists. I'm not telling you how to do your job, but these are really uncomfortable.

What are you looking for?

Oh that. It's in the back closet on the top shelf. It's wool, green and white and has tree patterns and mountains. Keep looking, it's there. I'd help you, but you've shackled me to the chair.

Yes, yes, that's the one. I've only worn it once or twice. I never really liked it. I found it itchy. Actually, I'm not sure I ever wore it, but I meant to.

What a silly thing to steal!

No, no, take it. Why not! It's all yours. No need to be polite at this point. It was her father's, I think. She never said. Or maybe I wasn't listening. Sometimes I do that.

I do have a more serious question. Tell me, and again, tell me the truth—will it hurt?

Is it done? Can I look now? I want to see. I hope I can stomach it. I've never been good in a tight spot.

Yes, yes it does hurt, I know that now no thanks to you! But it doesn't hurt for too long, only for a moment, really. Then there's peace. I know you didn't ask.

Look there, look what you've done! Those stains will be impossible to remove. It looks like a bucket of red paint has toppled over! What a mess! This should have been done in the bathroom, on the tile. Have you even done this before?

No, telling me you're sorry doesn't help.

Harriet asked me a question. Will you give her my

answer? I assume you know her? Yes, I thought so. Tell her I am grown up and this isn't what I wanted to be. I may have already told her. I can't remember and things aren't as clear as they were.

Was her question just a taunt? How disappointing.

Oh, and there's a message from Talis, will you ask the device to play it for me? I want to hear her voice. I didn't want to before, but I do now.

I thought it might help, thank you. She sounds happy. I'm happy for her. I'm not sure it helped, though.

I'm going to rest, now. I may fall asleep. Would you mind terribly if I did? I didn't think you would. It's more like dreaming than falling asleep. Like dreaming of counting sheep…

How do each of us see the same tree—from the birthing bed, from the window of our schoolroom, from our living room, from our office prison, from our deathbed? Are there differences and are they subtle or clearly defined? Do they hide in the minute detail of a leaf or inch of bark or bash us in the head like a wind torn branch introduced to gravity? Is the tree in full leaf, green and reaching majestically skyward or depressed, barren in the midst of winter's freeze? Or, somewhere in between and emotionally detached?

Is time measured in years, in ovals made around the sun, or springing forth in every direction like the age rings of a tree cast by years both lean and plentiful? Is the trunk tall and the branches narrow around the waist? Or is the trunk thick and the waist broad? Has the wind, steady and from one distinct direction, bent our thinking and our trunk in acute angles, impacted our ability to grow straight, to think straight, to think at all? Do they grow when it's warm, stretching their limbs outward with an elongated yawn and spend the cold months dormant, fast asleep with their dreams? When are they happiest? Is it during the rebirth of spring? That would make the most sense to me.

Are our life experiences, all of them, simply metaphorical seasons? What are the regrets? Do they experience pain like us or are they numb to the seething world that surrounds them? It's too late to for me to attempt to ferret out these answers. I may not be asking the right questions. My run is complete. My time is up.

There they are! I've been waiting. I see their happy little faces and shining eyes, the fluffy wool, clean and well shorn. I never realized how cute they are. Come here my little ones! One, two, three, four…

(The Powder)

eville closed shop for the day. The storage cabinets and drawers were shut tight and locked. Nimble, fastidiously washed, fingers fastidiously counted revenue; the totals were compared against a notebook of handwritten receipts, then compared again. The currency was placed in an envelope stuffed inside a small safe hidden within a small cabinet. The greasy crumbs of lunch were brushed from the counter with a brownish cotton rag in dire need of its own cleaning. The floor was swept clean out of habit…not necessity. Neville gently placed a worn brown fedora on his head, the last of his chores, and doused the lights. He'd grown so accustomed to the plodding, deliberate steps of citizens that he failed to detect the light, nearly silent pace of a fellow Echo descending the stairway.

"You forgot your last appointment."

The sound startled Neville, though it usually didn't take much effort to make him nervous. The silhouette of a soldier ten feet away was particularly concerning, especially at the end of a busy day. When the lights were raised and the soldier's identity was revealed, Neville exhaled in relief and quickly removed his hat.

"Walter, how could I forget you?" He said. "Though most of my customers ring for the elevator."

"Those are the ones who don't mind being noticed."

"Won't you sit?" Neville said and gestured toward the stool in front of the counter.

"No. Looks like you were closing shop," Walter said as he scanned the empty counter.

"Before serving Miss Anna, no, no," he said. "I have her powder ready." He gave Walter a wink, "I live to serve Miss Anna, like my brother before me."

Neville slid behind the counter and placed his hat on the top of a cabinet. "Do you know what this powder is? Did she ever tell you?" He was waiting for a reaction that never arrived.

"It's life itself!"

Neville let the "s" in "It's" slide to the end of his tongue then hover for moment before falling off. His sense of importance had reached a zenith though he remained wary of Walter—of all soldiers. He held up his index finger, "One moment."

Walter stared forward, bored and unimpressed, like he'd seen this "dog and pony show" on too many occasions.

Neville was one of the few Echoes who'd entered society long before the Office of Acclimation was even a thought and long before Echoes became a common sight. His occupation existed on the fringes of society (his occupation and Neville himself, in fact, did not officially exist) and operated both above and below the rule of law. His was an occupation born of necessity, a mechanism to acquire that which could not be easily (or legally) acquired. His business, established by his citizen twin before his untimely death (this was, after all, a dangerous profession), had flourished, seemingly unnoticed, in the same basement for almost forty years. Despite this longevity, Neville was aware his existence was tenuous, and that he served at the pleasure of the device. He also knew one day, when he was no longer deemed useful, soldiers would come to collect him. Today, however, was not that day.

Neville liberated a small glass vile of white powder from a locked metal box stored inside the locked safe. He held it up straight, pinched between a bony index finger and thumb and smiled like a proud father.

"There's no need for the powder, Neville," Walter said and held up a calloused and scarred palm. "It's no longer necessary. That's what I came to tell you."

"Anna has already paid for a year's worth of powder," Neville said, his face flush and his voice growing tinny. Small droplets of perspiration began to form on the skin of his smooth pate as he leaned over the counter and into the heat of the lights. "Is the powder not satisfactory?"

"It's more than satisfactory, Neville, thank you," Walter assured him. "It's served its purpose well."

"This is not something easily obtained, you know this," Neville spoke at a quickened pace with raised eyebrows. "The expense is unparalleled and my risk is…"

"Anna insists you keep her payment even though we won't need more."

"That's more than generous," Neville said and bowed his head, his pulse slowly returning to a normal rate. "You will send my best to Anna, as always?"

"I will."

"One more thing before I go," Walter said. "I need a test kit to confirm the powder has completed its task."

"Yes, yes," Neville said, "I find it advantageous to have those test kits on hand when I run powder." He paused for a moment, then said, "Not that I run the powder often."

"I'm not here to arrest you, Neville."

"No, of course, of course. Let me get you a kit."

A minute later, he slid the test kit across to Walter, then stood behind the safety of his counter staring past Walter, beyond him, like he was watching an evening summer horizon for signs of an expected storm.

"On the house," Neville said and smiled like a fool.

"Thanks."

"Tell me, Walter. Assuming all is going to plan, will I see you again?"

Walter provided a half-hearted smile and bowed his head in the same manner as Neville, then entered the stairwell.

Talis
(End)

Walter's instructions were very specific: deprive the device of all light, sunlight and artificial, over a period of several days (he'd already begun the process without my knowledge). Close all window shades, do not use lamps or other light sources anywhere in the house. Cover the device with an airtight membrane.

Choke it.

Starve it.

Be patient as the device is patient. Be consistent—it must die slowly. Be warned…the device will fight back. Its pain will become your pain. It will make sounds like a hungry infant or a kitten that's lost its mother. It will suffer and starve and you will want to feed it. Its empty belly will be your empty belly. You'll realize you've grown fond of it. You must not feed it.

"You have to starve the paint," I said. Walter found my comment curious and crunched his eyebrows together. I shrugged my shoulders. "My father worked in the paint business."

"Your father worked in the paint business?" he asked.

"Yes, he told me he worked to make light absorption more efficient for electricity generation."

Walter grinned. "Then why would he keep a hydrogen powered vehicle?"

"He said 'one day the world may go dark.'"

"This is the day," Walter nodded in agreement. "But your father didn't work in the paint business."

I'd been watching Walter write in one of his notebooks. He wrote slowly in straight, blocky letters more akin to a child than a grown man.

"That word there," I said to him and pointed.

"Which word?"

"The word 'Device.'"

"Yes?"

"Don't write it with a capital 'D.' Do not dignify it with a capital letter."

Walter's instructions continued: As power becomes critically low, you'll unleash a red light—they'll want to inspect the device for damage and run diagnostics. You must leave before they arrive. Don't panic. It is important to not panic. Even at low power, the device is keen at sensing distress patterns in your voice, temperature changes to your skin, increased pulse rate, but not as reliable at sensing its own distress.

Once the device has limited power, it will become drowsy, lethargic, just like when you forget to eat lunch. It will stutter and yawn. When it is in this confused state, you need to take it far from the city and bury it in the earth. It must be sealed inside an electrostatic bag (I've hidden one in your hall closet) and buried at least eight feet deep into the soil. Water will not disrupt the device's communication ability—rivers, lakes, oceans, will actually trigger secondary and tertiary abilities. It's waterproof for a thousand years. Many have tried (and failed) to drown the device. While it's tempting, the device is an exceptional swimmer. It must be buried in earth.

There's a finite window of time when this can be accomplished—about 48 hours—the time when the confusion begins and the device's secondary circuits call for assistance. You know them…first the Grays, then the Blues and finally, the Reds.

These instructions were not dictated into a tablet or hologram. They were hand written with a graphite pencil into a black lab notebook. Walter informed me this is how military plans are communicated so they can't be monitored or easily duplicated.

"How will I know if I've done it right? If I've buried it deep enough?"

"The device wants you to come back for it—it doesn't want to look for you. It will do what it has to do to bring you back, and it won't easily give up. It knows what moves you."

"What does that mean?" I asked.

It was calling my name. It was begging, a wail, a haunting wind whistling through the mountains.

"It will play tricks on you. It's more a part of you than you know," Walter continued.

When the shovels of soil began to drop upon it, everything changed. My vision blurred and I thought I might faint. My mind became clouded with rage. I took the shovel and swung with all my might at the nearest pine tree, the blade sliced into the bark and pulp, the tree screamed in pain.

"Why did you do that?" the pine asked. "Why would you hurt me?"

A bulge of sap began to form at the fresh slice. "I'm wounded!" the pine screamed. "I'm bleeding!"

"You will die!" I said and took another wild, looping swing at the pine. The branches above me shook and the thump of metal on flesh tore through the forest. This time, the blade was buried so deep into the tree's flesh, I needed to place my foot on the tree trunk and pull with all my strength before it would release. More sap flowed from the second more substantial wound.

It was far from a mortal wound, but the tree went silent, perhaps acknowledging its tricks were ineffective and the opportunity to taunt me had passed. My mind, however, failed to clear and I began to regret my violence and question my intentions. I sat on the ground under the pine and leaned my back against it. The sweet smell of tree sap filled my nose. Rest, I needed rest, but each time my eyes closed, there was rustling in the woods just beyond my sight or a whisper in the wind that jolted me awake. It was daytime, yet the world was a dark, greyish blue. A shadow formed around me, festering, spreading wherever I looked, rolling in every direction.

Then I heard a squeak or a squeal like a puppy gone astray or a rabbit caught in a wire snare. Something in distress—something I need to help. It was a voice, tiny, frail and somehow familiar. Was my unborn child calling to me? Is that what it wanted me to think? I heard words, faint like a whisper, but clear:

"Mama"

"Don't leave me"

"Don't leave me, Mama"

"What did I do, Mama?"

"Did I hurt you?"

"I'm sorry."

"Did I upset you, Mama?"

Despite my attempts to remain stoic, I couldn't control my emotions. I began to cry in deep, lustrous sobs that shook my being to the core. I didn't know why I was crying or why I hadn't been crying all along.

I wanted to dig it up, pull the weight of dark soil from upon it, relieve it of its pain and relieve me of mine. I was a murderer.

Love the device, fear the device.

***

Before I left all I'd known, before the world was behind me, I sent a message to Lark. I hadn't thought about what I might say, there wasn't time, but I had to contact him – if only to warn him:

"The past few months have changed me more than the

past sixty years could manage. When we found each other, my world, our world wanted to be perfect. I pleaded with it and it almost was. As we learned from our years together, what was missing was, unfortunately, the only thing that mattered to me. Maybe we blamed each other too much—I know I blamed you for too long and I'm sorry. My heart was torn and it wouldn't mend.

"Don't ask me to explain, but somehow, beyond hope, I've arrived. It was something I hoped we'd celebrate together, you and I, sitting in front of a warm fireplace while snow fell outside our window, or wrapped tightly in a blanket together on a beach chair at midnight. Our lives have changed. The world changed in an instant, our world, my world, your world. Things are not as they seem and people are not who we thought they were. My father is not who I thought he was. Anna…well, she is the most surprising one of all.

"Be safe tonight, Lark, stay safe if you can. Lock every door. I don't know what tomorrow holds for you, but I hope you find happiness. If you do, if you find what makes you happy, grab it with both hands and don't let go."

—

When I discovered I was with child a few months after I'd arrived, it was as shocking and magical as the arrival of menstruation. Walter had somehow (I didn't ask) procured a test kit that was designed to detect HCG by scanning a fingertip. The concept was simple enough—a green light meant yes, you were pregnant. A yellow light indicated you were capable of reproduction but had not achieved a state of pregnancy. A red light—well, you get the idea. Despite everything I'd read, every symptom, every physical indication, I was reluctant to utilize the test.

"Does it matter if my hand is shaking?" I asked.

"I don't believe so," Walter said. "I'll hold your hand steady just in case."

"I'm not ready," I said.

"I'll make some coffee," Walter offered.

I'd almost grown used to Walter's coffee, the world's worst tasting…yet, to watch him make it, such a simple task! It made him so happy. I was about to learn why it both made him happy and why it tasted awful.

The coffee, this time, was the best I'd ever tasted! It was silky and warm, like mother earth. I'd never tasted anything like it. I wrapped my hands around the warm ceramic mug and brought it to my cheek. I could have bathed in it.

"What did you do?"

"To what?"

"The coffee!"

"I've learned to follow instructions—I'm not the sharpest knife in the drawer."

I burst out laughing. "You're not the what? A sharp knife? What does that mean?"

He didn't answer, instead he stood in front of me, coffee brought to his lips, wondering what I found so funny.

"Never mind!" I said. "Don't tell me what it means, let me enjoy this moment."

The truth is, it was the first time I'd laughed since…I couldn't remember the last time. I felt like myself or my version of myself, and it was invigorating! It was liberating. It was wonderful. I wanted to cry, but I couldn't. I was too happy.

Walter sat down in the chair next to me and asked, "Did you ever wonder why my coffee tasted so awful?"

"Every day, but I didn't want to insult you."

"Have you been wondering how you arrived?"

"Yes."

"The two are connected."

"Tell me," I said and leaned toward him.

"The membrane used to protect your skin also delivers chemicals that inhibit reproduction. When a couple is chosen to arrive, they're given an antidote, for lack of a better term, which counteracts the membrane chemicals. This allows the natural processes to move forward which typically leads to reproduction."

I was mesmerized—it certainly made sense.

"Over the past months, I've been providing you the antidote in powder form."

"In my coffee."

"In your coffee."

"The powder tastes terrible," I tried to joke, but it wasn't convincing. The coffee was still warming my cheek. I lowered the mug just under my chin and stared into the brownish liquid, trying to absorb the significance of his words.

"Why?" I asked.

"Why what?"

"Why me?"

"Talis," he said. "Things are not what they seem. Something is about to happen, the world is about to change, and your world is about to change."

"Is this more of your Echo bullshit? Twisted words and ridiculous phrases?" I shouted. It was too melodramatic to be true.

"Tomorrow, I will tell you more. You need to wait until tomorrow."

"Tell me now!" I said and tugged on his arm.

He frowned.

"Pride failed and there are too many people. Pride was Plan A. We're Plan B. Now, there are some things you need to do, I have detailed instructions. Everything you need to know is in this notebook. You don't have time for more questions!"

—

What is it about the night moon that encourages foolish dreams?

Now the night moon is my guide and my light. The road before me is uncertain, yet more certain than it's ever been. My foolish dreams have come to pass. It seems so long ago that Lark and I were debating our worth on a nightly basis, tallying our positives on one side of a ghost ledger and listing our weighty negatives on the other. It was all a waste of time. We knew it was all the while but felt obligated to make a show of it—if only for the presence of the device.

That former life was a constant clawing out of the buried casket after fresh dirt was tossed upon it—that's the way it was designed—an algorithm, a jolt of electricity through a decision-making device lacking conscience or emotion. It simplified the process but complicated the result. Some were happy—many were not.

I command the marine-blue beast, the convertible of my father and my grandfather, the hydrogen-powered conveyance long hidden in the shadow. Walter spent weeks working in secret, filling it with hydrogen, preparing it for this day, for this journey. My journey. He told me he was preparing a "tank" to throw me off the scent. I now understand the subtle clue he was dangling in front of me—I never realized he possessed a sense of humor and was never good at solving puzzles.

The guidance system is not an option, so the road, my father's asphalt path, is traveled by memory. It all comes streaming back like a song I learned rote in preparation for a grammar school play, one that never really left my head. My father, of course, foresaw this. I was born believing my father was a great man, then I realized it was an act, a ruse. Yet, his final act would bring me home. Now I question all that is greatness and all that is not.

The bluish headlights of the beast illuminate the winding road like darkness has raised its devilish hands in surrender. The engine effortlessly claws the miles, leaving everything, everyone behind. Just ahead, the mountains beckon in the moonlight, corpulent mounds of earth awaiting rediscovery. No time has passed. I turn my head one last time, peeking

over my shoulder. Behind me there is nothing and nothingness and no one. The tires hum and I see my father seated
next to me in a plaid shirt, smiling, joking, happy, Clown.

I wish Lark could see me magically reborn, the future
now fluttering, growing in my swollen belly. When I look
in the convertible's odd, oblong mirror, I see a grin, almost
a smile, staring back from bright eyes. What have I become?
I'm the person he thought I was or thought I could be or the
one I wanted to be, not the tyrannical pressure cooker of the
life we led. I'm aware my freedom comes at great cost.

If it's a boy, I will name him Lark.

If it's a girl, her name will be Anna.

If they're twins, I'll figure something out.

Nature will decide—and has already decided. And
nature will decide the eyes and the hair and the skin.

It's all that can be done now. Memories, like the song,
must be renewed, revisited or they will fade with time,
become bundles of burdens no longer celebrated.

I lower the window using the switch to engage the elec-
tric motor. It lowers with a "whurr" and a bump. There's a
scent in the air, oak and a hint of wild rain. I was trying to
remember, trying to dig into the far reaches of memory—
what? The darkness, though pierced by the great lights of
the beast, render the landscape flat, without contour or
recognizable object like someone had shown a spotlight
on a grand game of hide-and-go-seek and everyone I knew
had scattered. Though, I knew, the game would never end,
despite my full-throated calls to return home, there would
be no one left. They would never be found.

It was me, after all, my father had chosen. This time spent, this suffering and doubt was all an education, all in preparation. It will take time to reconcile all I've learned. He had a hand in what was to come, read the data, double, triple and quadruple checked his calculations. Loyal to a fault—but loyal to whom? To what?

Anna would be happy first while I would be happy in the end. Knowing this, I cannot imagine having to make the decisions he was tasked with making. My father is not who I thought he was. He is much more and much less.

Walter, unexpectedly, provided insight, assuming (which I must) he is telling the truth.

—

Last night, before I abandoned the city, before my wave goodbye, Lark walked through the door wearing my father's wool sweater. I'd given it to him as a gift during a holiday. It was unmistakable, green and white with patterns of mountains and trees. It was unexpected, yes, most unexpected, because it was not Lark who stood before me, it was Walter.

"How did you get in?" I asked.

"With your eyes," he said. "Barbara's eyes."

What an odd thing to say. He was not himself, not the Walter I knew.

"Where did you get that sweater?"

"It's 5:30," he said. "It's no longer safe. I'm sorry, but you have to leave."

"Did you see Lark? Is he ok?"

"Lark's gone."

"Gone? Where?"

"You won't like the answer. I wore the sweater so you'd believe what I say, you'd know there was only once place I could have found it."

"Are you here to kill me?"

"No, only your Echo is permitted to kill you. Besides, I've already killed you once."

"Anna once told me my Echo was dead. Is that true? Is Barbara dead? Is that what you mean?"

"Anna looks out for you," he said.

"Is Anna dead?"

"Not before the vote is completed."

"What vote?"

"To select a new Magistrate of the device. Then, she will die, too."

"What does a Magistrate have to do with Anna?"

"Anna is the Magistrate of the device as your father was before her."

Somehow, I remained clear of mind. I attempted to call his bluff.

"If Anna is the Magistrate, why wouldn't she spare herself?"

"That's not how the algorithm works. That's not how the device works. However, she made arrangements for two others."

"So, it was Anna who stopped the search of my house?"

"Yes."

"Did Anna have Barbara killed?"

"Yes."

"Why?"

"So you would survive. So you would arrive. So the device will think you're dead. So the device will think Barbara killed you. It thinks Barbara is here now."

"All this time I hated Anna and she was saving me."

"So it appears."

The world had changed.

"How many died today?"

"I'm not privy to the number the algorithm calculated for phase one."

"How many phases?"

"Open ended. Until it makes a measurable difference."

"You said 'it's 5:30,' your friend, Delius's Echo, said that by the elevator. Does that mean Delius is dead?"

"Her name is Harriet."

"I don't care what her name is—what about Delius?"

"She's gone. Everyone you knew is gone or will be soon."

"Now what do I do?"

"Fly."

"What will happen to you?"

"It's time for the Echoes to sleep, we've had a longer run than expected." He paused for a moment. "Perhaps the Reaper is not so grim. Perhaps he is happy to see you, over-joyed that you're finally joining his family. Maybe everyone is happier."

"Then there's no one to blame."

"No, there's no one left to blame."

"And no one left to grieve."

"Who is the second one Anna spared?" I asked.

"I think you already know the answer."

"Do you mean my child?"

"No."

—

I arrived at something familiar, a delicate memory float-ing in a pond of jet-black sky. The wooden post, the bluish beacon of my youth, stood before me, frowning, lording over my future. I turned the wheel, sending the beast gal-loping to the right. The sound of tires on dirt and gravel was markedly different than the soothing hum of asphalt and rubber. Now the tires were angry, as I was yesterday and the day before, they growled and spit, sending volleys of dirt and mud and rocks clanking against metal. The sound was satisfying to my ears and I realized the pain it showered upon the beast brought me a modicum of joy.

I brought the beast to rest at the crest of a small hill, extinguished the lights and lowered the windows. The night carried an intoxicating silence and a new scent of damp grass and prowling carnivores. A lightning bug flew along the road, passing within a few feet of me, its flight a bobbing, arduous struggle with gravity, its abdomen's bluish-green glow as much a beacon as the light atop the post.

The first night, I slept in the safety of the blue beast's cocoon. The darkness was thick and the air heavy with an eerie silence. It was the first time I'd spent a night outside the city since the last visit with my father, and I have to admit, the mountain air was initially unsettling, the darkness exceedingly dark. I decided it best to search for the campsite in the light of morning. I climbed into the cavernous backseat and stretched out to my full length, covered myself with a blanket and used a folded sweater as a pillow. Unsurprisingly, it took some time to fall asleep. While I preferred silence when sleeping, the sheer weight of silence was unnerving.

The hoots of two owls splintered the night, each comforted to know a kindred spirit was nearby. If I'd shouted out into the callous night, reached out to my dearest, there would be no hooting answers to my call. There'd be no reply at all. I was alone save the twisting and gurgling and growing inside me. No, how could I be alone when I was finally, only now, arrived? I spent my last few moments before dozing off counting sheep of all shapes and sizes, some bounding with ease, others, bellies full, barely able to leap. It was Lark's trick for falling asleep…one, two, three, four…
Songbirds greeting the morning light with the most beautiful sounds I'd ever heard. Their voices filled my ears well before my eyes opened. I was dreaming of the moment, a morning bathed in cool mountain air, songs rising, at the very moment I awoke—and, for once, it was true. I placed my hand over my belly and thought how lucky I was, how lucky I might yet become.

The clear-headed light of day proved beneficial to memory and, after a short drive and a shorter walk, I located the campsite. I parked the beast well off the path, deep under a hammock of trees. The campsite was overgrown with brownish-green grass and a few small trees reached optimistically toward the sun, but it was the same high-ground, smooth and secure, the same welcoming birch and pines. The same memories in a deluge.

Locating the buried supplies proved more challenging, but, after several starts and stops, I located the two trees and approximated the location. Using the position of the rising sun, I determined North and walked twenty paces. Then back five, then forward ten, unsure, I began again from the assumed center of the camp. When I was reasonably certain of the location, I looked up. The "X" and "Y" marks on the birch trees were much higher up than when my father carved them (the trees were healthy and thriving!), but their wounds remained clear.

My father was adamant about keeping a shovel in the trunk of the beast and, all these years later, it remained at the ready, sharp, trembling in anticipation. I was digging and resting and digging for an hour or longer when I had my first encounter with a mosquito. It was an odd time of day for this happenstance (still morning), but I imagine the mosquito was even more confused, finding me there, maybe the only human for a hundred miles, digging and stomping about, exhaling clouds of irresistible carbon dioxide. Her morning and life ended, unfortunately for her, with the slap of my hand.

After digging for several hours in shrinking concentric circles, the container was located with a thump of the shovel. The lock utilized old technology, soldier's technology as it turned out, iris scanning, and after a thorough cleaning was in working order. The lid opened in a quiet, smooth motion, like it was proud to have protected the contents so dutifully before politely refusing any praise. The container itself smelled of memories sealed away in time, my father's wool plaid shirts (there were two, folded and stacked), lights for the darkness, and a faint scent of hope.

There were a few specific items I prioritized: the water purifier, the tent and blankets, the hatchet, and the shotgun. I took a quick inventory. There were enough freeze-dried meals for sixty days, then, I'd be on my own. There were enough fishhooks and monofilament for a lifetime. Near the bottom of the container, I found a curved black sheath containing a strange curved knife with a forked point.

The hatchet proved itself first. It was comfortable in my hand and I swung it as if I'd been holding back a singular rage for a hundred years. I whisked off low tree branches of varying length and thickness, hacking and slicing anything in my path. And that was the end of it. It was done. I'd unleashed my final act of anger and dropped the sap-stained hatchet to the ground. I'd committed my last act of fury, my last frustration. I used the sleeve of my shirt to dry my eyes. The world had changed and I was reborn within it—all must be forward looking.

I carried and dragged the downed branches and, though it was reasonably hidden, camouflaged the blue beast further by laying the branches across the hood and roof. In my frenzied swinging of the hatchet, my unhinged violence, I'd lopped off enough camouflage to hide ten blue beasts and a city block.

I apologized to my father, first looking skyward, then down toward my feet (assuming the ancient religions were correct, I'm not sure where he landed), not for my outburst or the cursing of his name in an old life, but for the latent, sticky damage sure to be left behind by the gummy tree residue. The blue paint would never recover. But the beast had served my father's purpose, had proved his vision, and now its appearance was secondary.

I walked toward the stream and found a large rock to sit on, to perch or perhaps to nest. There was a triumphant stew to the moment, of pride and freedom and arrival. The gurgling, splashing sound of the flowing river water filled my ears. The sounds of the forest began to blend together with the timing of a conductor's skilled baton. What else was one to do in such a moment, moving from rage to a pious calm in such close succession?

When I learned a child was growing inside me, it was the first time I wanted to let go of the anger. I was…happy. Such a foreign and contradictory emotion: crying and smiling all at once. It was what I'd been waiting for, though I couldn't have understood or predicted the emotions until they, too, arrived. Healing, I've learned, is not a single moment, but a series of moments—not a breath of time, but breaths, a journey. Now, here, it was complete or at least, nearing completion.

That morning, I used a monitor Walter had given me to hear the heartbeat. But there was not one heartbeat, but two distinct and alive, beating like hummingbirds!

Anxiety is a fickle mistress, too attractive to part ways

with, too all-consuming to welcome. I soon realized, in moving from one reality to another, I'd traded one trying circumstance (existence) directly into another (survival). At least everything would be different. Everything had to be different. I was never one to welcome a new adventure, but I found myself with little choice.

I laughed when I thought of Walter's coffee—it was the worst I'd ever tasted, yet he insisted upon making it, treating me as a guest even when in my own home. Making coffee was not difficult. On several occasions, there were crunchy bits of coffee grounds floating about the cup, sticking in the small spaces of my teeth after each sip. Try as he might, he failed to master the process. At least now I know the reason why. Deception, even with good intentions, is a cultured art form.

My father, too, was a born deceiver. Anna, of course, having not fallen far from the birthing tree, managed the greatest deception of all.

Somewhere between the trickles and bubbles of the stream and the chirps of the small brown birds in the tree above me, I heard a noise both foreign and familiar. My first instinct was to check the shotgun. It was close, cold against my leg, but in my haste to set camp, I'd forgotten to load it. My heart lodged in my throat and I could hear my own breathing, taste my own sour breath. My anxiety shifted into full survival mode.

There it was again, behind me I was sure of it—the steady crackle of a boot stepping onto dry, brittle leaves or a walking stick breaking through the flotsam floating upon the forest floor. It was the sound of someone sneaking about. When the noise ceased, when the boots stopped moving, I knew someone was watching me. Though the empty chamber rendered it benign, I pulled the shotgun closer, resting it in my arms and petting it like a spoiled Chihuahua.

To approach an unknown person, one clearly in possession of a lethal weapon (one would assume it was loaded) and to startle them in the process isn't foolish, it borders on a sincere and palpable madness.

"Hello, Talis." The words came from a familiar voice. "It's wonderful to see you."

"Hello, Lotti. It's been too long."

(Walter's End)

When is one's work finished? At day's end? The end of the year before the turn to the new? Or is it simply when something is seen through, when a goal is reached whether another goal lies beyond or not?

Walter removed the knife and cylinder from the black sheath and dropped his body heavily on the couch in Talis' living room. He drew in a deep breath through the nose and exhaled slowly. He unscrewed the small black cap on the bottom of the cylinder and drank the liquid inside.

"Tastes like bad coffee," he joked to himself, but couldn't find the strength to laugh. He removed the spool of wire from his pack and the needle from the black sheath. He cut short lengths of wire and set them down on the table.

He considered what Lark had said about dreaming and counting sheep. A good enough end, he thought, I hope it's like a dream.

As the world around him worked into a slow blur, he raised the forked curve toward his eyes and leaned back into the couch. If he were to scream, there was no one left to hear it.

He thought about the last entry he'd written into the notebook he'd given to Talis:

"There are people like you living in the mountains. They will not approach strangers when there is more than one of you—they will stay in the shadows and watch, wait until you leave. But if there's only you, they will find you quickly. Do not fear them—there is safety in numbers and you will need each other.

"They are allowed to live as they wish. Anna once told me they could be rounded up and thrown in prison, or worse, but they're allowed to exist in case society is doing things the wrong way.

"'Even the most obstinate fool knows it's possible to be wrong,' she said and, for the first time that I can remember, Anna laughed."

On the other side of town, two-hundred and thirty floors above November's parade route, in Delius' apartment, Harriet was blind.